stealing Home

NICOLE WILLIAMS

NEW YORK TIMES BESTSELLING AUTHOR

Stealing Home

ISBN-13: 978-1-940448-12-1 | ISBN-10: 1-940448-12-3

chapter *One*

WORKING FOR A professional baseball team was going to be the end of my love life. The past two years confirmed that theory, as had the last text I'd received from my latest *ex*-boyfriend.

Half of the year on the road added to another half of the year working grueling hours that rivaled a doctor's first year of residency equaled a whole lot of no free time to fill with a social agenda. Since being hired on by the San Diego Shock this season and the San Francisco Kings the year before that, the longest relationship I'd maintained spanned eight weeks.

This last one had barely cleared the four-week mark.

My lifestyle was costly, but it was worth it. Baseball was in my blood, and sports medicine was in my heart.

I'd grown up in a small Midwest town where people still got together for potlucks and everyone from the town hermit to the mayor attended a funeral. Where the only place you were expected to be after church on a Sunday was stretched out on the bleachers around the baseball field. It didn't matter if it was a T-ball game or the high school championships—the bleachers were always packed.

Baseball was a religion where I grew up—it was stitched into the fibers of my life—so it was no surprise when I ended up with a baseball player. No, the surprise came after I'd followed him to college and found him in bed with someone else.

It had taken the wind right out of me, along with my tendency to trust first and doubt after. Ben had been sleeping around for a while by the time I found out—friends had known and said nothing—and that was the day I made a promise to myself to never let another guy hurt me as he had, to never be made a fool of like that.

After changing schools mid-year, I started studying sports medicine and never looked back. Or at least not often. I only looked back when I found myself feeling something similar to what I'd felt for Ben. The relationship never lasted long after that.

As evidenced by my newest failed relationship.

"Whose ass do I need to kick, Doc?"

Dropping my phone into my lap, I looked across the aisle to see who was sliding into the row across from me.

Luke Archer.

Known to fans as the best hitter on the Shock, if not in all of pro baseball. Known to women for his good looks and up-to-no-good smile. Known to *Cosmo* magazine as being voted the Finest Ass in professional baseball. And known by the athletic training staff as a well-rounded pain in our asses.

Not because he thought he knew better or was yet another prima donna—which the sport had no shortage of—but because he held to the old-school code of taking care of an injury by "walking it off." If that didn't work, then we could usually convince him to pop one or two pain relievers after the game, and sometimes, if he was feeling especially accommodating, he'd accept a bag of ice.

Luke Archer was the real man of steel, and no one to date had managed to convince him he was also made of those injury-prone materials known as flesh and blood.

"Doc?" Archer's voice broke through my haze of thoughts. "Just give me his name and I'll take care of it."

The rest of the team and staff were shuffling down the aisle between us to find their seats on the team jet, but his stare aimed my way felt unyielding.

"What makes you think anyone's ass deserves a kicking?" I asked.

I returned a high-five as Reynolds passed by. He'd twisted his ankle in the game earlier today, and I'd been the first on the field to get him taken care of. I'd been the last one out of the locker room to finish getting him taken care of too. As a noob, I had to work twice as hard. As a woman, I had to work ten times as hard.

"I have three younger sisters. I have more experience than most with guys deserving ass kickings."

The last of the guys wandered by us. Without the break of their bodies coming between us, Archer's stare became too intense. His eyes seemed capable of pinning me to the back of the seat.

The head athletic trainer, Dax Shepherd, attended to

the "money" players—the ones like Archer, who brought fans to the stadium and were a large part of the Shock's impressive win-to-loss ratio. Up until this very moment, I didn't know Luke Archer was aware of my existence on this team or the planet.

"You really have three younger sisters?" I asked.

Unlike most of the female populace, I didn't know every last fact about Luke Archer. The news about his parents had made headlines a few years back, and that was all I knew about his personal life.

"I really do. And I talk to or text all of them every day."

"Plus you kick asses for them."

Archer's hazel eyes lightened. "Plus that." He twisted in his seat so he was almost facing me, his eyes dropping to the phone in my lap. "So? No one messes with my sisters. And no one messes with my team."

My forehead creased. "I'm not one of your teammates."

"You're a part of my team. Just because you don't play the field or swing a bat doesn't mean you're not. You keep us healthy and strong out there." When I cocked an eyebrow, he added, "And when we get injured, you make sure we get fixed up quickly so we can get back to doing what we love. You're every bit as vital to this team as . . ." He glanced up and down the aisle like he was looking for someone to fill in the blank with.

"As Luke Archer?" I completed for him.

His answer to that was a lifting of his eyes. "I'm one man who can swing one bat."

"One bat really, really hard. And very, very exactly," I interjected.

He continued, "You make sure twenty-five men can keep swinging their own bats."

"Well, there's me, the two other athletic trainers, the physical therapist, the personal trainers, and the actual doctor who help out with that too. I can't take all of the credit."

"Come on. You work twice as hard as any of them, so you should at least take most of the credit." When his phone started chiming in his slacks' pocket, he pulled it out, turned it off, and hid it back in his pocket.

"And since the closest Shepherd and Coach Beckett have let me get to you is handing out a water bottle, how would you know that?"

He pointed at his eyes. "I've got two of these and use them for observation on occasion."

"When they're not searching for your next conquest?" I gave an internal groan the moment after I'd voiced something that should have stayed unsaid.

My relationships with the players had always been professional and rarely, if ever, delved into the realm of personal information. If it didn't have to do with preventing or tending to injuries, I didn't bring it up.

Until now. When I'd just suggested that Luke Archer had a reputation in every city the Shock had visited, every hotel they'd stayed in. Perfect way for my first real conversation with the star player of the team, and the whole of professional baseball, to go.

Archer stayed quiet, studying me with that tipped

smile he was famous for.

"You know my opinion on rumors?" he said a minute later.

I was capable of nothing more than shaking my head.

"That they're started by haters. Spread by fools. And accepted by idiots."

My head tipped. "Are you calling me an idiot?"

His eyes flashed. "Are you calling me a manwhore?"

I studied him lounging in his seat with his legs kicked out in front of him, his wide chest stretching beneath his suit jacket, his long arms resting on the armrests.. His body was enough to weaken the resolve of someone as jaded to player *players* as I was, but his face didn't play second-string.

Brown hair lightened by the sun, smooth skin darkened by it, a strong jaw, and hazel eyes that trended more toward the green end of the spectrum; Luke Archer was quite possibly the most attractive man I'd ever laid eyes on. According to *Sports Anonymous*'s random poll of five thousand women, he was *the* best-looking guy in professional sports today. The other few billion women on the planet would have agreed with that title, I assumed.

"Do you always take so long to answer a question?" Archer motioned at me, waiting.

"No," I said, recalling the last question he'd asked me. *Snap out of it.* "I don't think that you're a . . . manwhore," I whispered the last part.

I'd had enough experience with the rumor mill to be a sympathetic party to the target of so many. Being one of the first and only female athletic trainers in professional sports had opened me up to a hundred rumors when I'd been hired. All versions of them had to do with me fucking my way into the position.

"Good." Archer nodded, seeming satisfied. "Because you certainly don't seem like an idiot."

"Thanks?"

He nodded again. "Welcome."

That was when the pilot's voice echoed through the team jet, running through his usual spiel. We were leaving Tampa and heading up to Chicago. Now that the season was in full swing, I lost track of the cities we were leaving and the ones we were heading toward. All of my attention was focused on the players and getting them through the season as injury-free as possible.

"I'm still waiting for that name, Doc." Archer clicked his seat belt into place when one of the attendants stopped beside him, looking ready to strap it into place for him.

When she saw mine unfastened, all I got was a lifted brow and a pointed finger before she moved on to the next aisle.

"Oh, it's okay. He's not worth it." I lifted my phone toward him before dropping it in the duffel bag I kept on hand at all times. Bandages, tape, painkillers, and a small cooler of ice packs were always at the ready whenever I was with the team. "Any guy who breaks up with someone via text message isn't worth much."

"Really? Over text?" Archer's eyes narrowed. "That's the reason the ass-kicking was invented. For those types of guys."

I shrugged as the plane started to taxi down the runway, the interior lights dimming. "We haven't even been together a month. Truthfully, it lasted longer than I thought it would. This kind of lifestyle"—I twirled my finger around the airplane—"makes it difficult to sustain a long-term relationship."

"That's why I'm not a fan of them."

"Long-term relationships?"

"*Any* kind of relationship," he said.

I nodded my understanding. The players had it worse than the team staff. At least in terms of having to question if a person was into them for who they were or because of their job, and the fame and money that came with it.

"I'm either practicing for a game, playing a game, re-covering from a game, or fueling up and resting for a game. There's not time for much else," he said.

Leaning into my armrest, I realized how strange it was to be having such an easy conversation with Luke Archer. It felt natural, not forced. Most of the players would take a moment to chat with me about something game-related, but I was still the new kid on the block. I felt like I had to pass some test before they'd accept me as a member of the team.

Archer didn't seem to be of the same mind though.

"Yeah, I know. It's like you need to find someone who can just travel with you wherever you go, right?" I said, thinking how much easier it would to be in a relationship with someone I got to see on a daily basis without two computer screens.

"Exactly. Someone who understands the lifestyle. Appreciates the sacrifices you have to make."

My head fell back into the headrest from the inertia of takeoff, but I could still feel Archer's eyes on me. "Someone who understands that the job comes first. Someone who doesn't get insecure or jealous or bent out of shape that they get the few precious minutes in between the job."

When my head turned toward him again, I found Luke Archer staring at me with a kind of intensity I hadn't seen aimed my way in a long time. My breath caught, and even though the strength of his stare threatened to overwhelm me, I held his gaze.

"Someone who understands the game. The commitment. The time. The sacrifice. Someone who's as committed to it as you are." One corner of his mouth twitched, carving a dimple into his cheek. "It's not like you could ever expect to find a person like that sitting in the row across the aisle from you, right?"

chapter Two

"THEY'RE READY FOR you, Archer!" Coach Beckett hollered into the bowels of the locker room after shoving through the doors.

A chorus of whistles and catcalls circled the space, echoing off the concrete walls and metal lockers.

"I don't know what *Sports Anonymous* wants with your ugly mug when they could have mine plastered across the cover instead," Reynolds piped up above the din as Archer rose from the bench in front of his locker.

I was busy wrapping Hernandez's ankle on the other side of the locker room, content to leave as much space between Archer and me as a confined space allowed. We hadn't said much to each other after takeoff last night, but I could feel his gaze on me when he thought I wasn't looking. By the time we'd touched down, the energy in the air between us was so strong, I felt like I could stick my finger out and be electrocuted by it.

"It's because they actually want to sell magazines."

Archer flashed a wide smile at Reynolds as he headed for the doors. "And they're not shooting for Halloween yet. I'll let them know you're interested when they're ready to shoot the ghouls-and-goblins edition though."

Reynolds snagged a towel from his locker and lobbed it across the room at Archer.

"The pretty boy of baseball. How bad does having to wear that title suck?" Reynolds shouted, which was followed by a few more whistles.

By now, I was used to the locker room banter and usually blocked it out. I wasn't sure why I couldn't today, but I guessed it had something to do with the subject the banter was focused on.

"Not too damn bad considering the pretty boy of baseball also happens to have the best batting average in the league." Archer wagged his brows a few times before blowing an air kiss Reynolds's way and shoving the door open.

"Archer!" Coach yelled.

Archer paused in the doorway. "Yeah, Coach?"

"Take a trainer with you."

Shepherd snagged his duffel and jogged toward the door.

"It's a photo shoot, Coach. I don't think we need to worry about me pulling a muscle or spraining something."

"With the way this season is shaping up for us to go to the big game, you are not allowed to take a piss without a trainer within arm's reach, you hear me?" Coach pointed at Archer, his shit-kicking face drawing his forehead into folds. "I will bubble-wrap you myself if I have to, but I will not let anything happen to my clutch hitter." Coach paused, but we all knew better than to argue when he was like this. He'd been a part of this game for fifty years and had the wins and pennants to prove it. "Understood?"

Archer nodded once. "Understood."

Shepherd, who'd frozen in the middle of Coach's tirade, went back into motion.

"But I get to pick who goes with me," Archer announced. Even though I wasn't looking at him, I could feel his eyes on me. "Doc? Whenever you're done babying Hernandez, we've got a photo shoot to get to."

I felt every eye in the locker room drift in my direction.

"Doc?" Shepherd said, his eyes narrowing on me. "Are you talking about Allie?"

I withheld the eye roll. It was common practice for everyone to refer to each other by last name—from the players to the coaching staff to the medical team. Shepherd refused to abide by that unsaid rule when it came to me though. Pretty sure it was his way of singling me out, since I wasn't already singled out enough, being the one woman in the locker room with thirty to forty men. I knew Shepherd saw me as some kind of joke—like I had no place working in professional baseball. He was kind of a prick, but in this profession, I had plenty of those to deal with.

"Doc. Yeah." Archer shrugged, tipping his head out the door when I looked up.

"She's not a doctor."

I glared across the room at Shepherd as I finished taping Hernandez's ankle.

"She's got her doctorate in sports medicine and busts her ass taking care of us every day, which is more than the actual team doctor who is . . ." Archer's gaze circled the room, before landing on Shepherd. "Not here."

The team doctor traveled with us and attended games, but he had a more lax schedule. He might have had more schooling, but at the end of the day, it was the trainers who saw to the bulk of the injuries, both preventing and treating them. The doctor was around to write prescriptions and consult with on more serious injuries.

"Coach, you good with this?" Shepherd asked, his hands settling on his hips.

"Oh, get off your high horse, Shepherd. If Archer wants Eden to go with him, fine. I'd feel the same way if I were in his shoes."

"Because she's the only woman around?" Shepherd fired back.

I kept biting my tongue. I was the only woman around, and it didn't help that there was no mistaking my gender when a guy looked at me. I was on the petite size, which automatically made them all want to step in to help me get something down from a shelf or lift something that looked heavy. I was also on the curvy side, which meant their eyes were easily, and frequently, distracted. In an effort to combat my petite, curvy stature, I wore my light hair back in a ponytail and never wore makeup. It wasn't like I was trying to be one of the guys—I was just trying to fit in a little easier.

Coach fired another warning look in Shepherd's direction. "Because she's damn good at her job. *That's* why."

Archer waved at me. "Doc? If you don't mind? I'm in a hurry to get this over with."

Patting Hernandez's knee, I rose. He gave me a smile of thanks before I threw my duffel over my shoulder and jogged for the doors. Shepherd was glaring at me, but I ignored him. Archer was staring at me again, but I couldn't ignore him so easily.

He was wearing a worn-in pair of jeans that stretched across his thighs and backside nicely, a basic T-shirt, and a team baseball cap. He held the door open for me and started to move down the long hall like he knew where we were going. Which I didn't.

I spent my time in the locker room or the field. I wasn't sure what this photo shoot was for, where it was being shot, or what was involved. Since the game was scheduled to start in a few hours, I guessed we weren't going far, but who knew. The sponsorship deals these players got were insane, and for the top players, sponsorships could bring in more money than the paycheck they earned playing ball.

"So what are you sponsoring today? A sports drink, a cereal, or an insurance company?" I asked, having to take two steps to every one of his long strides. Archer was a good foot taller than me and fast.

"None of the above." When he glanced back and noticed me rushing to keep up, he slowed his pace. "Today I'm shooting a spread for *Sports Anonymous.* Only a limited number of issues will be printed, and they'll be auctioned off to benefit the children's hospital back in San

Diego."

I knew the hospital he was talking about. During the off-season, when I had more than three minutes in a row of free time, I volunteered there. It was a facility that didn't charge anything for families who couldn't afford it and provided top-of-the-line care.

"And before you get too far in your estimation of how much they're paying me to do this, I can give you the exact number." Archer lifted his hand, his thumb and index finger joining to make a circle. "Zero dollars and zero cents." He smiled, lifting the circle his fingers were making to his eye. He peered at me through it.

A laugh swept past my lips. "That's refreshing. Not a lot of people do something without first thinking about what's in it for them, you know?"

Archer stuffed his hands in his pockets, tipping his head at a crew of people up ahead who looked like they were expecting him. "The way I see it, I'm already living the dream. I get paid to do what I love."

"You get paid *a lot* to do what you love," I added. Last I'd heard, Archer was one of the top five paid players in the sport.

"I might be the only guy in this sport with hamburger tastes on a steak budget, but maybe one day I'll go crazy and buy a house or something."

My eyebrows came together. "You don't have a house now?"

"I have an apartment back in San Diego. Nothing elaborate, but it works. We spend so much time on the road that having the kind of sprawling estates some of the guys have and only getting to enjoy it a few weeks out of the year seems like a big waste. Plus . . ." Archer's speech came to a succinct end.

"Plus what?"

The crew of people at the end of the hall were opening up doors leading into a room, practically paving a runway for us. *Sports Anonymous* logos were plastered everywhere, from the carpet leading into the room, to the lanyards around people's necks, to the stickers on the side of cameras that looked to be filming us as we moved closer.

Luke Archer was a god in this world—it was easy to forget when he was walking beside me with his hands in his pockets and talking about apartments.

"Plus"—Archer shrugged, slowing down as we got closer—"you know."

"I *don't* know."

He exhaled through his nose. "*Plus* I don't want to live in some big house by myself. My sisters still live in our family home north of San Diego, and I don't want to come 'home' to no one. Until I have someone waiting for me, my apartment works just great."

His pace picked back up again, and this time it seemed like he wanted to put some distance between us. I could have told him I felt the same. I could have told him that that was the reason I was living in my own apartment back in San Diego. I could have told him, but something about the way Luke Archer looked at me made me wonder if keeping the private parts of our lives to ourselves was better.

I couldn't get involved with another player. Definitely not one on the very same team I worked for. People already talked shit about how I'd gotten here. If it got out that I was sleeping with the star of the team, no one would ever take me seriously again. My credibility as a damn good athletic trainer would be stamped out by the assumption that I did my best work on my back.

No. I couldn't get involved with a player.

One like Luke Archer especially.

chapter *Three*

THIS WASN'T THE type of photo shoot I was imagining. This was the hot baseball player equivalent of the *Sports Anonymous* swimsuit edition.

Thanks to my line of work, I'd seen more than my fair share of half to mostly to fully naked men. I didn't even blink when the full monty processional rolled out of the showers after a game. But for some reason, seeing Archer shirtless from a good twenty feet away was threatening to put me into cardiac arrest.

I'd never worked with him before, since Shepherd oversaw him, but when Archer had emerged from the dressing room a few minutes after being sent in there, I was relieved I hadn't. Holding onto my removed professionalism would have been impossible while working with Archer.

There were plenty of good bodies in this sport. Plenty of good bodies I'd had my hands all over. A good body didn't turn my head anymore. They'd become commonplace and everyday.

But Luke Archer . . . his body went beyond good and fell somewhere in the realm of unreal.

Muscles bulged from his shoulders down to his forearms, veins drawing jagged patterns down his arms. His chest was wide, narrowing into a stomach that was so cut, I found myself wondering how many women had fantasized about running their tongues down the canyons tapering into his pants.

The baseball pants they'd stuffed him in were at least two sizes too small, showcasing the ideal ballplayer's round ass, along with something just as prominent around front.

Shit. Checking out Luke Archer's package was not okay.

Other than the too-small pants, they'd provided him with a royal blue belt to match his stirrups, a flashy pair of Nike cleats, and they'd kept his team cap settled on his head, hooding his eyes just enough. I wished they'd turned it around because Archer's eyes held in the same theme as his body—unreal.

He had a baseball bat braced behind his neck, his arms curved around the back of it, while the photographer snapped photo after photo. How many variants of the exact same pose did they need?

"How am I looking over there, Doc?" Archer kept his eyes on the camera, managing to move his lips just enough to speak. From the number of billboards, magazines, and articles I'd seen him in, he probably had lots of experience honing the skill.

Taming my stare, I swallowed and shrugged. "Like you're the pretty boy of baseball for a reason."

His careful expression fell, his eyes cutting to the back of the room where I was hovering against the wall, pretending not to eye-molest him like the rest of the women in the room were. And some of the men.

"Ouch, Doc. You got anything in that magic bag of yours to fix a bruised ego?"

"An ego your size?" I fired back. "Not likely."

"Double ouch." He spun the bat over his head, watching me.

"But I do have a tin of eye black." I shoved off the wall, unzipping my bag. I dug around inside for it. "That should be up to the task of dirtying up a pretty face."

No one stopped me as I moved in front of the cameras toward him. The photographer quit firing photos like he'd poured milk over his speed pills for breakfast to see what I was up to.

"My face is not pretty." Archer juggled the bat from hand to hand, almost smirking at me as I moved closer. "It's rugged."

After unscrewing the tin, I dragged my fingers in the eye black and paused before lifting them to his face. When I got a "go ahead" hand twirl from the photographer and a couple others from *Sports Anonymous*, I drew a streak down the side of his face. He didn't blink as he watched me draw another line down the other cheek. Dipping my fingers in again, I swirled even more on before painting a thick streak down the side of his neck.

I kept my attention on what I was doing instead of

who I was doing it to. I focused on moving my fingers instead of what my fingers were moving against. The heat from his skin was transferring into the pads of my fingers, cresting over my body from his chest.

What am I doing? I was an athletic trainer, not a body paint expert.

Then I spun his cap around so his eyes could be seen better. Eyes like those should not be shadowed by anything.

"There," I said, almost a whisper. "Now you're rugged." For the first time since I touched him, I glanced up to find him studying me.

His pupils were dilated, his breaths coming faster through his just parted lips. "You missed a spot."

Grabbing my hand, his fingers laced through mine as he swirled both of our fingers through the tin. Guiding my hand back to him, he settled our fingers on his chest, drawing a thick line diagonally across it. I didn't miss the pace of his heart as my fingers skimmed over it. It was going faster than normal, but not quite as fast as mine.

He trailed our joined hands lower, sketching a streak across his stomach. Then another down his stomach. All the way *down,* until the tips of my fingers brushed the nylon of his belt.

When a shiver trembled down my body, he didn't miss it. Knitting his fingers tighter through mine, he grinned down at me.

"Yes, that's perfect." The photographer leaned back from his camera, examining Archer with a fist tucked beneath his chin. "I love it. Bidders will go nutso." Then the photographer waved his finger between Archer and me. "And you know what I'd love even more? Her in your jersey."

My head was already shaking as I started to step away.

Archer's hand pulled me back to him. "I love that idea too. Doc in my jersey." His gaze skimmed down me, lingering on my thighs. "In *only* my jersey."

chapter *Four*

NOTHING BUT A couple pieces of underwear and a certain number 11 jersey with the name Archer stamped across the back were all I wore.

I still didn't understand why I'd gone along with his crazy scheme, but I was pretty sure it had something to do with this shoot being for a charity that was near and dear to my heart . . . and the way Archer's eyes had softened when he asked me for the tenth time. Although by then, he was more begging than requesting.

They were waiting for me. I could tell because it was quiet out in the main part of the room, other than the metallic ting of the baseball bat Archer was probably clinking against his cleats. The game was starting in two hours, and I still had a team to get loosened up and warmed up.

Closing my eyes, I psyched myself up as best as I could before slipping out from behind the curtain sectioning off the dressing room.

Everyone turned to look.

But it was Archer who was staring.

As I padded across the room, he turned so he was facing me, refusing to discipline his stare. His eyes roamed down me, lingering on where the bottom of his jersey brushed across my thighs. When he licked his lips, his stare unyielding, I felt the band of muscles circling my stomach tighten.

"I am never going to be able to look at that jersey the same way again," he said.

I kept moving closer, slowing when I was a body's length away from him. My face was hopefully giving off an unaffected vibe, though everything behind it was the opposite.

"I'm going to need that back once you take it off."

My vocal cords constricted, but not before I squeaked out one word. "Why?" I cleared my throat and tried again. "You've got two dozen of these things back in the locker room."

"Yeah, but none of them have been bundled around your body. I want this one for tonight's game." He pinched the sleeve of the jersey, inching me closer. "It will bring me good luck."

Luke Archer was fucking with me. I didn't know why, but he was. I didn't know his intentions, where his teasing originated from, or what he had in mind from here, but I knew I should back away instead of letting him pull me closer. I knew I should turn my back and go back to the way things were before Archer had turned his attention in my direction, but one could not simply turn and walk away when a man like him was looking at a woman like me the way he was.

It was a universal principle.

"If you don't mind, we really need to get this shoot wrapped up before Coach Beckett storms in here and breaks another camera over my head." The photographer came up behind me, dropping his hands to my shoulders as he positioned me in front of Archer.

"He replaced the last camera he broke of yours, right?" Archer asked, the smokiness clearing from his expression.

"Sure, yeah, but he can't replace my sense of safety as easily."

The photographer and Archer exchanged a look while I stayed quiet and let him position me. Coach Beckett was one of the best in the league. He was also one of the most hot-headed.

The photographer slid me to the side of Archer just enough that I wouldn't be obscuring too much of his body, which no doubt would drive up the auction price. "Yeah, that's nice."

I didn't know what they needed me here for—Archer sold himself just fine—but when the photographer nestled Archer's bat behind my back, stationing Archer's hands at the base and top of it, I knew escape wasn't part of the plan. Not with the way Archer was drawing me closer to him, cinching the bat tighter against my back.

"Why don't you put your hand right here on his chest, and tip your head just enough we get a profile of that stunning face?"

Before the objection could rise from my throat, Archer shook his head. "No, she doesn't want her face showing."

The photographer paused, giving us a curious look for a moment before wandering back to his camera. "Fine, fine. Whatever she's comfortable with."

"Thank you," I whispered up at him, still not sure how I'd wound up in Luke Archer's jersey and pressed up against his body, posing for a cover that would probably sell for thousands a pop.

"You're welcome." His bat tightened against me a little more, its cool touch seeping through the material of his jersey and the warmth of his skin creeping through the front of it. "But I'm pretty sure no one's going to be able to recognize your hand, so assume the position." His gaze dropped to his streaked chest.

My heart thudded against my sternum at the firmness in his voice. At the glint in his eyes. "When we're done with this pose, I'm going to suggest a different one. Where you get to 'assume the position' of bending over and I pretend to shove this bat up your ass."

Archer gave a low whistle. "Shit, Doc. If I'd have known you were into the kinky stuff, I would have found some way to get you in my arms with nothing but my jersey on sooner."

When the photographer announced he was going to commence shooting, I turned my head away, focusing on the space just over Archer's shoulder. "Because you knew I existed before last night, right?"

"I've known you've existed from the first day you walked out onto the diamond at spring practice." He was back to barely moving his lips, managing to hold a sexy-as-hell smirk as he stared at the camera.

"And why was last night the first time you ever said anything to me?"

His eyes darted my way for a moment. "Because you didn't seem like the type who was open to mixing business with pleasure, and I respected that."

"That's why we're in our present situation?" I glanced down at myself, where his jersey was floating a good foot above my knees. "Because you respected my policy on that topic?"

The corner of his mouth twitched, the lights of the camera flashing in his eyes. "Hey, even a patient man has his limits." With that, the position of his bat moved so the end of it was nuzzled into my backside. Which meant his fist curled around it was all up in my butt's business too.

His crooked smile became more pronounced.

The photographer whistled, I guess approving of whatever feedback he was getting on his end of the camera. "Every woman in America wants to be you right now, sweetheart."

Archer grunted, his knuckles digging a little deeper into my ass. "More like every guy in America wants to be me right now."

I did my best to stay still and, you know, keep from hyperventilating. The heat from the lights, combined with the heat spilling from his body, was stifling. With his cleats on and me being barefoot, Archer seemed that much taller. With my petite body pressed up against his, his frame seemed that much more imposing. With his arms snug around me, I could feel the strength he possessed. It was the kind that was meant for power. The kind that told me he could do anything he wanted to me and I'd be helpless to stop it. It was thrilling at the same time it was terrifying.

A few minutes later, my heart still thudding so hard I prayed he couldn't hear it, the skin between Archer's brows creased. "When will the magazines go up for auction?"

"In two months. Don't worry, we'll send you one." The photographer continued to snap photo after photo.

"Yeah, I'm going to need more than that."

"How many more?"

The crease deepened. I was trying to keep my head turned away from him, but my eyes weren't so capable of the task.

"Eh, thirty? Maybe forty? Just enough for every wall in my apartment. Don't worry, I'll pay whatever the auction price winds up being."

My forehead creased. "Every wall in your apartment?"

"I like my name on your back."

The way he said it, like it should have been obvious and required no explanation, made me smile. "Such a caveman."

"If I were a caveman, I'd tell you where I'd rather have my name on you." Archer's fist pressed into my backside enough to smash me closer to him. "*Tattooed* on you so you couldn't just take it off or wash it off."

"Wow, okay, so I retract my former accusation in favor of labeling you some barbarian-Neanderthal-caveman hybrid."

"Before you form any more unfavorable opinions of me, let me just remind you that I'm a baseball player." When I arched a brow at him, he continued, "I'm good with my hands, know what to do with a big stick, and am used to getting dirty."

I had to bite my lip to keep from smiling. I didn't want him to think I found any of what he'd said endearing, even though I kind of did.

With my hand tucked behind his back, I pinched at his side. "Only in baseball is someone highly skilled if they hit one third of the balls thrown in their direction."

His plastered on smolder fell when he shot me a wounded expression. "Sure Coach doesn't have you around to keep our egos in check?"

"A pro baseball player's ego? No amount of insults could keep that in check." I felt my straight face falter as he threw me another injured look.

"Triple ouch."

"Oh, please. You like it."

"Yeah"—he tipped his hips into me just enough—"I do."

I nearly leapt through the ceiling when I felt him hard against me, but I recovered. Eventually.

"Everything okay?" the photographer asked, not sounding like he really cared.

Archer waited for me to answer.

"Everything's great," I muttered.

"Thanks. I get that a lot." Archer's eyes were spilling

amusement.

Grumbling under my breath, I did my best to stay cool and collected through the remainder of the shoot. I felt the opposite though. In fact, I felt my own arousal wetting my underwear. Shit. My body was responding to his. Of its own accord. Without my permission. Feeling him hard and ready against me should have made me want to turn and run. Instead, my body was doing the opposite—welcoming him and inviting him closer.

After a minute, Archer must have noticed the frustrated look on my face. "Sorry," he whispered.

Even hearing the softness his voice could attain, feeling the heat of his breath on my cheek, made my body weaken.

"Sorry for what?" I asked. "That I'm wearing nothing but your jersey? That I somehow wound up in this photo shoot when I had no idea I'd be posing for *Sports Anonymous* with Luke Archer? Or are you sorry for your erection you clearly can't control when I'm stuck sandwiched between you and a baseball bat?"

Archer lowered his head so his mouth was beside my ear. "I'm sorry if my 'erection' makes you uncomfortable."

"But not sorry because you have one, right?"

His head shook slowly. "No, not sorry for that."

"Of course not."

When he shrugged, the band of muscle beneath his chest moved against my hand. "At least now you know."

"At least now I know what?"

"How I feel."

I blew out a breath. “Yeah, I have a really good idea how you *feel*. Thanks for clearing it up.”

The harder Archer fought his smile, the more pronounced his dimple became. The auction price for these issues just spiked a grand or two. The children’s hospital could thank me later.

“You know how this game works. I know how.” He paused, letting that settle in the space between us. “You just have to decide if you want to play.”

“Because you have decided?”

His bat pressed deeper into my back, drawing me impossibly closer to his body. His arousal settled hard into the side of my stomach. “Doc, I’m already playing.”

chapter *Five*

DID I WANT to play the game?

That was the question that had been playing on repeat through my head the past two weeks. I still hadn't arrived at any answers though.

For as strong as Archer had come on, he'd backed off to the point of simple formalities. I wasn't sure if that was his way of letting me work things out without any pressure from him or if he'd lost interest or if, hell, I'd imagined everything during that twenty-four-hour period.

Either way, I was still considering my answer. *Do I want to play the game?*

Typically that question would have been followed up with an immediate and inviolate no. But this wasn't the typical guy asking. It was Luke Archer. It wasn't the name or prestige that came with the name that had caught and kept my attention; it was the man behind the name. He was a good one—a decent one.

Now that I was watching Archer through a different

lens than the athletic trainer one I'd observed him with before, I was noticing new things. Like the way he always made it a point to take time before and after a game to sign autographs on kids' baseball gloves or balls or napkins or whatever they waved at him from the fence.

Or the way he embodied the role of a team player—never showboating after nailing a ball over the fences, never failing to pat a teammate on the back when they trudged back to the dugout after striking out.

Or the way he was the first one on the field to warm-up and stayed after to help pack up. As star athletes went, he was the only one I'd come across who didn't behave like a star.

In terms of men to get involved with, he seemed like the best kind a woman could hope for. I just couldn't decide if this woman was ready to get involved with anyone, especially someone on the same team. Especially the star player who had no lack of scrutinizing eyes and rolling cameras aimed his way at any given time.

No matter how discreet we tried to be, someone would always be watching. Someone would find out. It was inevitable. And I couldn't risk getting caught sleeping with a player when I'd already had to fight tooth and nail to get noticed on my own merit.

I couldn't afford to be that athletic trainer who'd clawed her way into the pros by clawing her nails down Luke Archer's back. Was a few weeks or months of wild abandon with Archer worth the risk of losing all my credibility?

My frustrated groan rolled down the hotel hall as I

stormed down it some time after two in the morning. I'd never been much of a sleeper, and ever since Luke Archer's roundabout proposition, sleep had been that much harder to attain.

The exercise room was open twenty-four hours a day, thank god, because I needed to work out some serious pent-up energy. We had a big game tomorrow against the Orlando Rays, and everyone was on edge. On edge translated to being ripe for injury, which translated into the athletic training team being extra busy tomorrow. The Shock and the Rays were rivals, but that rivalry ran deeper than most rival relationships did. The players couldn't stand each other, and the last time Reynolds's nose had been broken was during a game against the Rays. I didn't know where the rivalry came from, but I was dreading tomorrow's game.

Waving my cardkey beside the exercise room keypad, I could just make out the whir of a treadmill behind the door. I'd been hoping I'd have the room to myself, but it sounded like someone else was an insomniac.

I threw open the door, moved inside, and stopped short. If the room hadn't been lined with mirrors, I might have quietly backed out and found another way to vent my excess energy, but it was too late. Archer had already seen my reflection in the mirror in front of the treadmill he was running on.

A slow smile shifted into place as he lifted his hand in a wave.

The door clicked closed behind me, sealing me in that small room, alone with him. The scent of sweat and man was overwhelming, rolling over me in heavy waves. I wasn't sure if this was what scientists meant when they talked about pheromones and their effect on the opposite sex, but shit, my body was practically writhing from the scent of Luke Archer filling the room.

The view of him didn't help either.

"Couldn't sleep." Archer pulled the ear buds from his ears, glancing at me over his shoulder.

"Yeah, me either."

"I don't sleep for shit most nights, but it's been impossible lately."

I could feel his eyes on me as I moved across the room, grabbed one of the folded towels, and brought it over to him. He was drenched with sweat, beads of it rolling from his hair down his forehead. The rest of his body was just as soaked.

That tended to happen when a person was maintaining a . . . I leaned over the treadmill just enough to read the screens.

"Archer!" I chided, going into athletic trainer mode instantly. My finger punched the speed down until he wasn't sprinting at speed Super Human.

He grumbled as he wiped his face with the towel. "Sorry, Doc. I didn't think you'd be around to catch me in the act."

"The act of running ten miles per hour for the past . . ." My eyes darted to the time screen, widening instantly. "Hour?! You've got a big game tomorrow. What were you thinking running—no, wait, *sprinting*—almost ten miles less than twelve hours before it starts?"

Archer sighed when I kept punching the speed down, but he didn't fight me on it. "I was thinking I couldn't sleep and had about ten miles of wind-sprint energy to work off before I could even try."

"There are other ways to work off energy that don't involve you going into cardiac arrest or passing out from the effort."

"Those are my favorite ways to work off energy actually." He ran the towel through his wet hair, sending beads of sweat raining down onto my arm.

The room was warm and I was hot, but I still got goose bumps from feeling Archer's sweat spray on my skin. It made me think of other ways it could happen. It made me fantasize about those ways.

Clearing my throat, I reached for his water bottle—which was empty—and backed up for the water cooler. "No more ten-mile dashes the night before a game. You're going to hurt yourself or wear yourself out. You need a way to burn off some extra energy, I'll work up a plan that doesn't involve you setting speed records on a treadmill, okay?"

"Would this plan have anything to do with you and me horizontal in my bed?"

Two weeks of silence on the issue, and now he was jumping in with both feet. I guessed I could rule out his interest passing or it all being some figment of my imagination.

"Archer," I said in warning while I filled his water bottle.

"Fine, fine." His feet continued their steady pace,

pounding the treadmill. "You and me vertical up against my hotel shower wall?"

Another round of chills spiraled down my spine. He knew just what to say to make my body respond. He knew just how to say it to test my willpower.

"I take your silence to mean you haven't arrived at any conclusions regarding you and me?"

My head shook as I filled his water bottle.

"Have you given *any* thought to you and me?"

He watched me as I screwed the bottle's lid back on and wandered toward him. "Lots of thought."

"And?" He took the water bottle from me, waiting.

Looking at him from this close was hard. Seeing him shirtless again made me remember the way his body had felt against mine during that impromptu photo shoot. The way his hard planes accepted my soft curves. The way his arms felt around me, tucking me close to him like nothing could get past him. God. This wasn't supposed to happen. Not with him. Not with a player on the very team I was working for.

"And it will require lots more thought," I said, picking up his bottle and holding it out for him with a raised eyebrow. Gauging how long he'd been running and how much he was sweating, he needed to down a couple of liters to restore his fluid levels. I needed to make sure he got some electrolytes in him too.

"Anything I can do to help sway your decision?" Archer looked down at me while he sucked on his water bottle. He gave me a *happy now?* look when he handed it back, almost empty.

"Yeah. Explain why you ignored me for months, then when you decided to notice me, you pretty much came on so strong it was like I was the last woman on the planet and the fate of it rested on our ability to procreate." I headed back to the water cooler, thankful for the added space between us.

He'd been guarding his looks around me when others were around, but now that we alone, he was staring at me like he knew me as intimately as two people could know one another. He didn't blink once, his long strides strumming along the treadmill. His muscled shoulders lifted. "I go after what I want. I don't leave you guessing. Or wondering. With me, you get what you see. You know what I want. Who I am."

When I handed him the fresh water bottle, he drank a few more sips before squirting a stream onto his head. I backed up into the wall behind me. Distance seemed like a good thing when Luke Archer was looking at me the way he was, saying the things he was, sweating and breathing hard the way he was.

"And you want . . . *me?*" I said, needing the words spelled out.

He didn't pause. His stride didn't lose a beat. "I do."

My heart felt like it was climbing into my throat. "Why?"

His gaze pinned me to the wall. "Because you know the demands of this lifestyle. You're as committed to your job as I am to mine. You're as interested in keeping this quiet as I am." He motioned at me like I was living proof of his confession. "I respect you as a trainer and a human being. And, most importantly of all, I am attracted to you in a way that makes it hard to breathe when you're close." That was when he paused to take a breath. "I want you in a way that makes rolling into bed every night without fantasizing about crawling over your body impossible. That's *why*." He let that settle in the air, never looking away. "I can't promise you forever. I can't promise any length of time actually, but I can promise honesty and commitment. The rest, I don't know. We'll just have to wait and see."

"And sex." My eyebrow lifted. "You can promise me that too, right?"

A tipped smile slid into place. "I can absolutely promise you that."

"Glad that's all cleared up," I muttered, wondering if anything was or if everything was just more confusing now. Was he suggesting a sex-only relationship? A no-strings-attached one? Was he hinting at maybe more?

Did I care?

My answer to that question was unsettling. So I shuffled it to the back of my mind.

"This schedule—this life . . . it would be nice to have someone to climb into bed with at night." His shoulders lifted as he kept clipping along. "To share private moments with. The same person. A person I trust."

I knew all too well what he meant. Ours was a lonely life. One filled with endless tasks, long hours, and hundreds of people . . . yet still impossibly lonely. It would be wonderful to have one person I could trust to share intimacy with. A person I could wrap my body around at the end of a long day and pretend that life was more than schedules and commitments.

"This is a strange arrangement," I said after a minute.

He was cooling down and needed to get some more fluids, electrolytes, and rest before tomorrow's game. The thing was, I didn't trust myself to go back to his room and follow up on those items. We hadn't even crossed a line yet and already I was letting my feelings for him get in the way of my job.

I couldn't do that. No matter where Luke Archer and I wound up, I couldn't let my feelings for him get in the way of my job.

"This is a strange life that we live," he replied, punching the treadmill to a stop. "When you make your decision, you know where to find me. You know where I stand. Let me know when you figure out where you do."

"No pressure, right?"

He stopped wiping off his face, his eyes darkening as he stepped off the treadmill and moved toward me. "Depending on your answer, there'll be plenty of pressure. In all the right places. Whenever you need it. Whenever you want it."

My legs squeezed together. "You really don't leave anything open to interpretation, do you?"

"No." His head shook. "Don't let the fear of striking out hold you back."

My tongue went into the side of my cheek. "I think Mr. Ruth was referring to baseball, not dating."

His dimple sunk into his cheek. "Maybe he was, but that's the principle Mr. Archer applies to all facets of his life." Backing away from me, he snagged his shirt off a barbell and took another sip from his water bottle. He was keeping true to his word—letting me figure this out without him pressuring me . . . yet.

The promise or threat or whatever it was made my pulse race. I could only imagine how much Luke Archer could pressure the hell out of me.

"Archer," I called before he slipped through the door. My job first. That was the way this had to work, no matter what my decision.

"Yeah, yeah, Doc. I'll down a couple electrolyte tabs and get some rest." He froze in the doorway, glancing back at me still pinned to the wall. "Unless you've made up your mind and have something else in mind for my bed tonight."

Lifting my hand, I waved. "Sweet dreams, Archer."

chapter Six

THIS GAME WAS going to come down to the last inning. I hated games like these. The players loved games like these though.

There was so much adrenaline and testosterone shooting through the dugout, we would be in trouble if someone lit a match. This energy was that explosive.

By the top of the fourth inning, two fights had already been broken up—one started by Reynolds when he claimed the shortstop from the Rays blew him an air-kiss after Reynolds tried to steal third, and the second when Garfield, the catcher, threw down with a player who got walked but decided to "accidentally" sail his bat into Garfield's chest pad.

Archer had sprinted from his position at first base to try to break it up and managed to get taken to the ground when a few players from the Rays fired out of their dugout, assuming he was joining forces with Garfield.

We'd be lucky to leave the field with everyone on

their own two feet instead of sprawled out on a parade of stretchers.

"Hey." Archer slid next to me on the bench after jogging into the dugout in the ninth.

"Hey," I replied, trying to ignore that same mix of sweat and man closing in around me when he slid closer. Along with it came the hint of grass and leather. It should have been offensive, but it was the opposite. I loved this sport and everything that came with it—the scents included.

"So how do you like playing football?" I asked, keeping a straight face.

"Please, football players have it easy with all that padding and protection. I'm going to look like I got tuned up by a tire iron tomorrow." He turned his forearms over, and I could already make out a few bruises breaking to the surface.

"You want something for the pain?" I reached down for my duffel bag.

"Do I ever want something for the pain?"

"Fine." I tucked the bag back under the bench. The bruises weren't bad—he'd survive.

"But I wouldn't mind a nice deep-tissue massage later. Let's say ten o'clock. My room. Clothing optional." He kept his voice quiet, smirking at the field as the Rays threw a few warm-up balls.

"No pressure," I said under my breath.

His smirk grew. "No pressure."

When Coach paced down the dugout past us, Archer casually shifted farther down the bench from me, his smirk fading.

"We're one down, boys. One down." Coach snarled at the scoreboard while Hernandez slid on his batting helmet and took a few practice swings out on the grass. "We're going to finish this game two up, you hear me? We're not going to tie. We're not going to win by one run. We're going to win by two."

A chorus of grunts of agreement echoed through the dugout.

"Let's remind these clowns they have no right to consider themselves baseball players. Let's show these damn pussy Rays that the Shock is made up of gods and legends." Coach snarled into the outfield next, like the sight of the Rays made him violent. "We don't just play ball, boys. We. Win. Ball."

Another echo of shouts fired around me, Archer being the loudest. The sound of him grunting and hollering beside me made me feel things in places I should not have been feeling when I was trapped in a dugout with a mess of stinky, angry ball players.

When Hernandez moved up to the plate, the team cheered him on while most of the Rays' crowd started heckling him.

Garfield was on deck, and Archer was in the hole.

"I want to steal home." Archer scooted back closer to me once Coach's and the other players' attention was on Hernandez stepping up to the plate.

"No one steals home anymore."

"Doesn't mean it can't be done."

His arm was brushing against mine, messing with my

head. "Doesn't mean it should be done either."

"We need a run. We need a big play." He sucked in a breath when Hernandez swung at the pitch . . . and missed. Strike one. "If Hernandez and Garfield can get on base and I hit a double or a triple, we'll be in good shape."

"Or you could just hit one of those homerun things you're setting records for. That could work." I glanced at him from the corners of my eyes.

He shook his head at me.

"Stealing home plate?" I repeated, realizing he was serious. "It's like a one-in-a-thousand shot you'll pull it off."

"Never tell me the odds. It only makes me want to do it more." His jaw ground when Hernandez chalked up another swing and a miss.

"Play it safe. I know you're favoring your right leg." My gaze dropped to his leg running down the length of mine. "I don't know what you did to it, but I know it's hurting. Don't risk hurting it any more." When his jaw set a little, I sighed. "Am I going to have to tell Coach?"

"I just twisted it weird. It's fine. A little ice and rest and I'll be good."

"Is this when you tell me you're going to walk it off?"

It wasn't affecting his performance much, but he'd need speed and luck to steal home. With the way he was favoring his leg, speed was not in his corner tonight.

"No. This is when I *show* you I'm going to walk it off. Right after I add another point to our side of the scoreboard when I steal home."

When Shepherd glanced down the bench, I reached into my duffel so it looked like I had a reason to be having a conversation with the star player. Instead of the real reason we were having a conversation.

"Don't steal home," I said once Shepherd's attention went back to the game. When Archer sighed, I added, "Not as in not ever. Just wait until the time's right. When you know you'll be successful."

He looked ready to argue when pitch number three sailed at Hernandez and he connected with the ball, sending a whizzing line-drive into left field. Hernandez turned on the jets and hauled to first base, making it right before the ball smacked into the first baseman's glove.

The dugout let loose with a round of whistles and cheers.

"I'm on deck."

"Good luck." I nudged his leg with mine as he stood.

"Hey, I've got my lucky shirt on. I'm all set." He slid off his ball cap and sailed it into my lap.

"Yeah, but it's been washed a few times since I was in it. Not sure how much luck's left in it."

"I'm feeling pretty damn lucky." He pinched at the shirt before slipping a batting helmet onto his head. "But don't worry. I fully plan on having my jersey draped around your body again soon."

My eyes wandered down the dugout. No one was watching—they were too busy holding their breaths as Garfield sauntered up to the plate.

"Don't steal home."

"Make me a better offer, and I'll consider it." He

paused for a heartbeat, challenging me with his eyes. When my lips stayed sealed, he climbed the steps out of the dugout. "Home plate it is."

Archer grabbed his bat from the rack, lowered into hitting position, and took a couple of practice swings. Even over the roar of the stadium, I could hear the air displaced from the power of his swing. All measure of lightness had faded from his expression—that iron resolve took its place. He had mastered a level of focus most of the guys in the game hadn't come close to yet.

While everyone watched Garfield at the plate, I watched Archer. I examined the way he held himself, the way he moved his body. Every movement was intentional. The way he commanded his body on the baseball field led me to imagine how he could control it in bed. It was impossible to conclude he'd be a sloppy, flailing lover who couldn't please his lover if the end of a revolver was drilled into his temple.

The crack of a ball connecting with a bat shook me from my reverie. The dugout exploded with noise again when Garfield sped to first base. Hernandez made it to second right before the ball sailed into the baseman's mitt.

"Come on, Archer!" Coach hollered as Archer stalked up to home plate. "Give 'em hell, son!"

My throat ran dry. Even when I swallowed, it didn't help. The crowd was really heckling now that the best batter in the league was stepping up to the plate with two on base.

Before he stepped into the box, he performed his ritual tapping of his cleats with his bat. Two taps on the left cleat. Three on the right. Then he rolled his shoulders a few time before stepping into the box and lowering into position.

The pitcher shook his head at the signal the catcher had just flashed him. He nodded at the second signal.

Archer drove pitchers up a wall because he didn't have a weakness. He'd swing at every type of pitch. He'd connect with them all too. Whether he swung or not had more to do with what felt right when that ball was launching his way—at least, that's what I'd heard him mention in an interview earlier in the season.

As the pitcher wound up, everyone in the dugout, including myself, sucked in a breath. The ball moved so fast I barely noticed the white blur sail through the air before the crack of Archer's bat connecting with it echoed through the stadium. The ball went high and deep. Everyone in the dugout stood up from the bench, and just when it looked like the ball was going to clear the fence, it clinked against the back of the fence and bounced deep into center field.

Garfield was already rounding third base and Hernandez was closing in on home before the centerfielder made it to the ball. As a testament to Archer's speed, even on a semi-injured leg, he was on his way to third before Garfield had barely passed it.

Coach Beckett was beating the ground in front of the dugout, and the rest of the players looked like they were ready to charge the field.

The third base coach waved Archer toward home, but it was a bad call. He should have stopped him. Archer had only made it halfway to home before the ball smacked into the catcher's mitt.

Archer lunged back to third, but not before the ball made it to the third baseman. He was caught in a hotbox, no sooner lunging for home before pivoting back for third.

The players in the dugout were roaring. Coach Beckett's shouts were drowned out by the noise. The whole time, I didn't think I took a breath.

Dust erupted around Archer's cleats with every step, clouding up the air around him. When he turned back toward home, he waited for the third baseman to launch the ball to the catcher before switching directions and hauling back to third. Only because I was watching Archer's face so intently did I see it—the flash of pain. No doubt brought on by the sudden twist in direction on the leg he'd been favoring for the past few innings.

Diving, Archer's arms wound around third base before the baseman's glove brushed him with the ball that had just slapped into it. The crowd around the stadium was booing their guts out as the ump announced Archer safe. The scoreboard changed to put the Shock up by one at the top of the ninth.

The dugout had turned into a clan of brutes beating their chests, grunting their approval, and adjusting their cups like they simply couldn't *not* fondle themselves after that kind of play.

I was already reaching for my bag and heading up the stairs before Archer stood. By the time the third base coach waved me over, I was only a few strides away.

The leg he'd been favoring earlier was the same one

he could barely apply any weight to now. The umps called a timeout in order to bring in a runner for Archer while the third base coach and I helped Archer off the field.

His arms draped around our shoulders as he let us help him.

"Don't put any weight on it," I ordered when I caught him trying to walk himself off.

"I'm fine." His fingers drilled into the outside of my shoulder as we moved him off the field. "I just tweaked a muscle or something."

"Or something," I mumbled, shaking my head.

Shepherd jogged up to take the third base coach's place beside Archer.

"Hey, don't worry. This is all part of my plan," Archer said.

"Part of your plan to get carried off the field mid-season?" I whispered as Shepherd and the third base coach exchanged a few words.

"Part of my plans to get my arms around you."

"You've got *one* arm around me."

"For now." His arm tightened around me as his mouth lowered to my ear. "But something tells me the second will be wrapping around you soon enough."

chapter *Seven*

"SHOULDN'T YOU BUY me dinner first or something?" Archer smirked at me when he lifted up onto his elbows as I tugged his sweats down his legs.

"Tell you what," I replied after I gave one last pull, freeing the dark gray sweats from him. After handing him a towel, I waited for him to drape it over his lap. Instead he curled it up and tossed it across the hotel room. "How about I draw you a nice, soothing, relaxing bath? Full of ice."

As I came around the side of his bed, it took all of my concentration to focus on the compress I needed to unwrap instead of what was resting just a little higher. At least he had underwear on, but it wasn't like they provided much coverage. Especially when what was tucked inside them looked about ready to burst free.

And dammit. I'd looked. From the way I could feel him watching me, he knew I'd looked too.

"Another ice bath. Sounds perfect. Since my balls

aren't already blue enough." Archer spread his legs open farther as I reached down to unwind the compress circling his upper right thigh.

"Yeah, well, that's what you get for not listening to the recommendation of your athletic trainer to take it easy." I unwound the bandage slowly, not wanting to further inflame the area. "Every three hours, we'll alternate fifteen minutes of ice and heat."

"Yay." He cleared his throat when my fingers brushed his inner thigh as I unwound the last of the compress Shepherd had wrapped back in the locker room after his first ice bath. "Since you got to decide on the ice option, how about I decide on the heat option?"

From the low notes in his voice, I knew exactly what he meant. "The plan is to calm the tear. Not further aggravate it."

"Okay. I can work with that." When I exhaled, he added, "I've got ideas."

"Ideas that involve what you have in mind and not using your groin muscles?" My gaze wandered back to that part of his anatomy. Right before moving onto a different part of it. *Holy shit.* Something about knowing he wanted me and wasn't concerned with hiding that desire made me dizzy. "Good luck with that."

Archer watched me as I disappeared into the bathroom to turn off the water filling the tub. "Never underestimate the ingenuity of a desperate man."

After testing the temperature of the bath, I grabbed one more bag of ice and dumped it in. I'd arranged to have four new bags arrive every few hours through the night so

I could mitigate the damage Archer's pulled groin muscle would have on his season.

The team doctor had done an exam in the locker room and assured Coach Beckett that with aggressive care these first twenty-four hours, Archer should be able to play the game in New Orleans three days from now.

From my own exam, I knew the doctor was giving Coach a serious case of lip service. The only way Archer would be able to play the Shock's next game was if we injected him with every illegal substance in this sport and on the market in general. It was a class two pull—no amount of walking off would fix this in a couple days' time.

"Are you hungry, Doc?" Archer called from the other room.

"That depends on the context of that question."

His laugh carried into the bathroom. "You know me too well. However, in this instance, I'm referring to hunger as in for food. The room service type specifically. I can order something for us so we can eat once you're done cryogenically freezing my gonads."

Wandering back into his room, I dried off my hands with a towel. "Hey, this isn't my fault—I warned you to take it easy."

I ceremoniously waved my arms toward the bathroom, feeling nervous. I'd given so many ice baths I could have filled an entire ocean with them, but this one was different. It was for Luke Archer. In his hotel room instead of the locker room. Plus, back there, the entire coaching and medical staff had been present, pow-wowing a plan of treatment. No one else was here now though.

Just me. Just him. And a locked door.

Shepherd had crapped a brick when Archer requested that I attend to him through the night, right before the suspicious look that shadowed his face insinuated the very thing I was trying to avoid. If someone on the team was already suspicious that something was going on between Archer and me and we hadn't even done anything, what chance did we have of no one finding out when and if we actually did?

"Dinner?" Archer waved the room service menu at me.

"I'll order it for us. We need to get you in the tub before you get any more swollen."

Archer's gaze swept down his body, landing on the very part of him I was trying not to inspect. "I can think of something to help with the 'swelling.'"

Crossing my arms, I gave him an unfazed look. "I'm here to see to your leg. Not your dick."

"I think that by taking care of one, you'll be taking care of the other."

"True. Ice baths are up to the task of tending to torn muscles and swollen dicks. So let's get started."

Archer lay stretched out in bed for another minute, calling my bluff, but when I made no move to throw myself at him, he sighed. "The ice bath it is."

"Good choice." Rushing to him when he started to climb off the bed, I positioned myself under his arm to keep him from putting any weight on the injured leg.

Archer's arm wound snuggly around me, holding me

close as we slowly made our way into the bathroom. "I could get used to this. My arm around you. You spending the night in my room. Getting my needs tended to by you. I might just try to injure myself again once I'm healed up from this one."

"Can't wait to run that plan by Coach," I muttered as we came to a stop at the edge of the tub. When he didn't step in right away, I lifted my eyebrows. "Afraid of a little ice bath?"

"Please. I've had just as many of these over the past five years as I have showers. I'm immune to them."

"Then what are you waiting for?"

His eyes lowered. "I don't know what you're into, Doc, but I don't typically bathe with my clothes on."

"Those aren't clothes."

"I don't bathe with my underwear on. That better?"

Before I could say anything else, his free hand tugged the waistband down over his hips. Then said underwear were in a heap at his feet.

"There. Much better." When he glanced over, he didn't miss my crestfallen expression. "Sorry? Did you want to help with that?"

My eyes lifted to the ceiling. Mostly just to keep them from exploring Archer's exposed body. "Get in the bath already."

I kept my gaze up as I helped him step into the tub, but even then, it was hard not to notice him in my peripheral vision. Even stepping into a thirty degree tub of water and ice, probably in serious pain from the muscle tear, he was still hard.

The muscles south of my navel contracted.

He didn't wince when his other foot stepped inside, the water skimming just below his knees. His skin didn't even erupt in goose bumps. Maybe he was immune to the discomfort of it all.

"Okay, lower down nice and easy. No sudden movements. Use me to brace yourself." I slid my other arm under his armpit to guide him down, but he was barely putting any weight on me.

"Thanks, Doc. I already planned on using you to brace myself later, but I appreciate the green light." His curved smile lifted even as the rest of his body lowered into the tub.

"Can you be serious for five minutes?"

Archer's jaw set when *that* part of him disappeared into the tub, but he didn't yelp or grimace like most of the guys did. "I *am* being serious."

"Fine, then can you not be *so* serious? I've got a job to do tonight, and it doesn't include fucking you." I blamed my blunt crudeness on the cold water and feeling like my eyes were going to go crossed from keeping them focused on the ceiling. "Besides, how can you even be thinking that with a groin pull?"

Archer worked his jaw loose as he lowered the rest of himself into the tub. Water sloshed up the sides as his body displaced it, ice clinking against the fiberglass. "I could be thinking that if my head had just been severed from my neck."

I smiled as I turned to grab a towel to roll into a headrest for him. "I'm starting to believe you could."

His eyes met mine as I leaned down, tucking the rolled towel behind his head. Archer wasn't the type who liked the extra babying and comfort measures, but I needed to keep my mind and hands busy. I didn't trust myself around him, and staying focused on my job was the only way to make it through the night without letting Archer take my body—the way I'd spent the past couple of weeks dreaming.

"So?" His voice was the verbal equivalent of a nudge.

My head shook. "No. We can't."

"Why not?"

That was the very question I'd been beating to death since Archer's attention turned my way. "You're a player. I'm on the staff. I think there's something in our employment agreements that strongly discourages, if not prohibits, relationships like the kind you're suggesting."

His head turned so it was facing me. His eyes were darker than I was used to seeing them—more gray than green. "No one would have to know."

As a distraction, I tested the water again. His hand floated up to the surface and found mine. Despite the freezing water, the warmth from his skin spread up my arm. "People would find out."

"Not if we were careful."

My fingers tied around his of their own accord. It was like a reflex—when Archer reached for me, I reached back. "People always find out."

"You and me. Those are the only people who will find out."

My eyes lifted to his. "And where do you see this relationship going?"

"Anywhere we want it to." When his body moved closer, a wave of water crested over the lip of the tub. "I can't promise you romance and forever any more than you can promise me the same. This life, it doesn't leave much room for anything but baseball, but I can promise you my free time when I get it. My attention when it's mine to give to something other than the game. My loyalty and devotion."

My mind traveled back in time to a place and a player who I thought had embodied those qualities. I'd been wrong. "Loyalty and devotion? Is a player even capable of that?

"This one is."

When his thumb brushed up my hand and circled my wrist, I felt a jolt spill down my back. A simple touch. An innocent one. Already my body was firing to life from this lightest of caresses—I couldn't imagine how I'd survive what he had in mind.

"I need time to decide. We've both got so much to lose. I can't just jump into something like this."

"How much more time?" Archer tugged my hand so I slid a little closer. "Because I'm pretty sure my manhood's going to be obsolete in about ten minutes."

I splashed some water at him. "For being such a tough guy, you're kind of a big baby."

He blinked the water out of his lashes. "Do you know how cold these things are?"

"Yeah, I played sports. I spent my fair share of time in an ice bath."

"And how long has it been since your last one?"

"A while," I answered.

"In quantitative terms?"

I paused long enough that a grin was already forming on him by the time I got anything out. "A while is quantitative enough."

"Well, I've already had two tonight and get to look forward to another eight in the next twenty-four hours." He sank deeper into the tub, but it wasn't big enough to fit his long frame. His knees popped out from beneath the surface of the water.

"Maybe next time you'll listen to me when I tell you to take it easy."

"Taking it easy isn't my approach to anything in life. Especially when it comes to baseball."

My gaze dropped to where his hand was still holding mine beneath the water. "I hadn't noticed."

"Good. Then this next part shouldn't come as a surprise." At the same time his hand tugged on mine, his other arm reached across the tub to wind around my back.

Before I'd caught up to the fact that Archer's arms were around me, I was being rolled into the tub with him. As my body crashed over his, water and ice surged over the sides, spilling across the tile floor as ice scattered everywhere. I was so surprised by what had just happened, the icy water took a few moments to process.

Archer must have noticed my face creasing into a grimace or felt the skin on my arms rising, because that was when he moved his hands to my waist, floating my body down over his lap.

The cold water was forgotten again.

His hands seemed to swallow my whole waist, his grip firm, his touch insistent. My chest started moving faster when I felt his hard length pressed between my legs.

"What are you doing?" I asked.

His fingers buried deeper into my body. "Making my move."

"In an ice bath?"

"On a fucking polar ice cap if need be."

Beneath my hand, I could feel his own chest moving faster . . . and how had my hand wound up there in the first place? I didn't remember putting it there.

"I need more time, Archer. You and me . . . I need more time to make up my mind."

He sat up higher in the tub so his face was almost level with mine. "You've already made your decision, Doc. You know that. I know that. You might not be ready to acknowledge it, but you've made your decision."

My head shook, but my other hand moved to him, forming around his shoulder. "What makes you so sure?"

"Because you're still in this tub with me."

"You're holding me here in this tub with you."

His hands fell away from my waist, but my body stayed hovering above his, my hands still formed around him.

"Because you didn't object when I said I wanted you to attend to me tonight."

As he said the last part, his hips flexed into me in such a way I felt heat that no ice bath could touch course through my body.

"It's my job to attend to you . . ." When one of his brows elevated, I clarified, "It's my job to attend to *the players*. How would it look if I said no when you told Coach you wanted me tonight?"

I was saying everything wrong. Everything came out sounding like some double entendre, but his body beneath mine made talking difficult. It made talking logically impossible.

"It would have looked like you didn't want to be alone with me. In my room. Because you didn't trust yourself to be alone in my room with me."

Making his point, his hands moved back to me. I'd let my chance to get away go by. His fingers pulled the back of my shirt free from my pants, his palm spreading against the freshly exposed patch of skin. His hand was searing hot, the kind of heat that felt capable of branding me.

"I don't trust myself to be alone with you," I breathed, his hand roaming higher up my back.

"Good." His throat bobbed as he swallowed. "I want to kiss you, Doc. Now. This would be a good time to tell me how you feel about the two of us."

My stomach wrung when his darkening eyes roamed my mouth. "One request."

"Name it." His words echoed off the tile walls.

"Stop calling me Doc. Kind of ruins the mood."

He fought a smile as his hand slid around the back of my neck. "Fine. *Allie*."

My body trembled when I heard him say my name. It quaked again when the hard heat settled between us pressed into the space between my legs.

"I want to kiss you. And after that, I want to do more." His hand at my neck drew me closer, water dripping down his lashes as his gaze dipped to my mouth again. "Allie."

My heart hammered in my chest as our mouths moved closer. I could feel the warmth from his breath breaking over my lips when I whispered, "And what if I don't want to kiss you back?"

"Then don't kiss me back."

His mouth covered mine then, succinctly silencing whatever objection was about to rise from me next. Successfully silencing whatever objection that could ever rise from me again when it had to do with Archer kissing me.

Luke Archer kissed like he played baseball—intently, skillfully, and like he'd spent his whole life practicing for this one moment in time. His lips tasted mine for a moment, testing me, before I felt his tongue slip into my mouth, teasing my tongue, until mine thrust into his mouth.

One kiss. One minute. I knew that if I let Luke Archer past my walls, he would consume me. I never would have guessed it could happen so quickly. So completely.

One taste. One touch. And he owned me.

Our mouths broke their rhythm just long enough for Archer to peel my wet shirt over my head. My chest crashed into his, sending more water and ice crashing over the lip of the tub.

His fingers worked my bra open and managed to slide it free without breaking our kiss. When my bare chest covered his, my nipples as hard from arousal as from the cold, something rattled deep in his chest.

"I need you." He breathed against my mouth, his fingers working at my pants.

My hand wandered down him, drifting into the space between us. When my fingers curled around him, that rattle in his chest echoed in the room.

"I need you , too," I rasped.

"Finally," he sighed.

"Finally?"

"I've been waiting for you to say that." As he lowered my zipper, his knuckles brushed down my panties.

"To say what?" I jolted when he pressed one of his knuckles into a certain place. "I need you? Take me now? Sorry I held out on you a whole two weeks. I know it's probably the longest you've had to wait for a girl to make up her mind on that issue."

His head shook, his eyes never leaving mine. "For you to acknowledge that you feel something for me too." His arms twined around my waist right before he rose from the tub, lifting me with him.

For the briefest flash, I remembered why I was there, and it wasn't just to let Luke Archer do whatever he wanted to my body.

"Your leg." Panic took my voice an octave higher. "Put me down. You shouldn't even be standing on your own right now."

"I'm not planning on staying vertical for much longer. Don't worry, Do . . ." He caught himself, clearing his throat as he stepped out of the tub with me still in his arms. "Allie."

"Put me down now, Archer."

"No."

"Dammit."

His jaw set as he held me tightly, my struggle to get free useless. "I will put you down when I'm damn good and ready to put you down."

"I'm supposed to be helping your leg get better. Not make it worse." I wiggled against him, but his grip was unbreakable. He had almost a solid foot of length and fifty pounds of weight on me. Not to mention a solid ton of resolve and determination. "Put me down right this second, or so help me god, I will change my position on the whole needing you in me stance."

"You can change your stance on the position all you want. I like them all." His hand smacked my ass when I continued to struggle against him. So help me god, if he injured himself even worse, I was not letting him out of an ice bath for the next forty-eight hours. "So long as I get to have my dick buried deep inside you, the position's of little concern to me."

His dirty words had my legs tightening around him even though I was still trying to pull away. "Let me go, Archer." My words came out slowly, as much an order as they were a threat.

"Fine," he fired back right before his arms freed me, sending me spilling onto the mattress behind me. The mattress whined as my body bounced onto it. "Now let's get these panties you've got in a serious bunch off of you."

Even though the material was pasted to my skin from the bath, Archer had no problem peeling my pants down my body in one quick pull. He threw them over his shoulder, sending them smacking into the wall behind him.

Staring at me spread below him on his bed, a crooked smile christened Archer's face. Something flashed in his eyes when they roamed my bare chest. When they roamed lower, his Adam's apple bobbed. "Your panties. Take them off."

My heart was about to burst out of my chest. What resided between my legs was pulsing with need. The rest of my body was bursting into flames, need fueling the fire.

Even through all of that, I was still pissed at him for not listening to me and risking injuring himself even worse.

"You don't listen to me. I think I'm going to repay the favor." My fingers curled around one of the pillows stacked on his bed, and I sailed it at his face.

Archer merely slid a little to the side and the pillow whizzed past him. "Fine. Keep them on. I can work around a little fabric. No problem."

When his hand dropped to stroke himself a couple of times as he stared at the area between my legs, my fingers found their way beneath the sides of my panties, pulling them down my hips.

"Shit, that's hot."

Finishing pulling my panties off my feet, I flung them at his face too. This time he didn't step out of the way.

"What's hot? This . . ." My gaze moved down to the freshly exposed part of my body.

Archer wet his lips when his eyes followed mine. "It's hot that I can tell you to do something and you do it.

That's hot."

His hands dropped to my bent knees, slowly opening them until he could step between them. His gaze never left the area between my legs.

"*This* . . ."—the way he said it, the way he was looking at it, made every muscle in my body tighten—"is the damn finest sight I've ever laid my eyes on." When my eyebrow lifted as I leaned up onto my elbows, he added, "Even better than the sight of that scoreboard at the end of tonight's game, or the scoreboard at the end of any game I've ever played and won." He didn't stop opening my legs until they could go no farther.

"Not sure how I feel about you comparing that part of my anatomy to a scoreboard, but I think you meant that as a compliment. So thanks?"

"Damn straight I meant that as a compliment." Archer yanked open the nightstand drawer and reached inside . . . only to find a hotel bible. "So not what I was looking for." He groaned.

"Conditioned response?" I said, touching myself as he rushed over to one of his suitcases by the door.

"More like some combination of wishful thinking and my dick using up the blood supply that normally carries oxygen to my head." When I raised an eyebrow at him now throwing things out of his suitcase as he searched, he tapped his temple. "This head."

"Ah, got it. So you keep condoms in your nightstand at home and your suitcase when you're on the road?"

"Hopefully," he said as shoes and shirts continued to tumble out of his bag.

"Hopefully?"

"More wishful thinking." His face lit up when he pulled what looked like a shower bag out of his suitcase.

I watched him, confused, as he tore the zipper open and spilled more things onto the floor in his desperate search efforts. I hadn't slept with many guys, but those few I had always knew where they'd stashed their condoms, almost like that little plastic square was an extension of their dick. In a way, I supposed it was. A guy could just as soon misplace his actual package as he could a condom when he was looking to get laid.

With Archer's blatant attempts to "woo" me, I would have thought he'd have a dozen stashed in a dozen different places, all within arm's reach at any given time. Why was he acting like he didn't have a goddamn clue where one condom was?

"Shit," he cursed under his breath.

"What?"

He upended his shower bag, shaking loose the last few contents. No small plastic squares floated out. "Shit."

Sitting up in bed, I inspected the mess he'd made ripping his suitcase apart. "You can't say shit twice and not fill the naked woman in the room in on why you're saying that."

His hands combed through his hair as he turned in a circle like he was looking for something. "Condoms."

"Yeah. I've heard of them."

His gaze landed on me. "I don't have any."

I swallowed. "Shit."

"My word exactly."

Now it was me digging around in the nightstand drawer, shaking the bible out just to make sure there wasn't one hiding in the pages. You know, since so many people probably used a condom as a bookmark while they were reading the good word at night. "Are you sure? I mean, you're Luke Archer. I thought you'd be on an automatic refill program or something. You know, where they drop a cargo box out of the air every month."

A dark brow lifted at me. "I'm sure. Do you have one?"

"Yeah, right here in my back pocket," I said, patting my bare backside. "Oh, wait."

"You're telling me you don't have a condom in that giant magic bag of yours?" Archer paced over to my duffel bag.

"Oddly enough, that kind of protection doesn't fall under my job duties."

He groaned like my answer was causing physical pain. "I could run out and get a box."

My head whipped with a firm no. "You are not supposed to be running anywhere. If anyone on the team saw you, they'd string me up." He shouldn't even be on his feet right now, pacing around like a crazed man desperate to unearth some condom cache. "Plus, I'm on the shot, so if you're worried about getting me pregnant, I'm covered." I cleared my throat. "In case you're worried about anything else, I'm good there too."

Archer's hands went to his hips, still pacing the room. "Yeah, yeah, I'm set there too, but I want to be careful. It shouldn't just be up to the woman to take care of birth control."

I sat up straighter. "Wow. You are oddly progressive for being such a Neanderthal."

"I could call Reynolds." He was already moving for his cell phone on top of the desk. "He has those things coming out of his ears."

"Yeah, because that would be a great idea." I deepened my voice a few notes before continuing, "Hey, Reynolds, can I borrow a condom when the only woman in my room right now is the team's athletic trainer?"

"That would imply that Reynolds has the mental capacity to put one and one together."

I gave that a moment's thought then shrugged. "Good point. Give him a call."

"No, you're right." Archer's head shook, sending his damp hair spilling across his forehead. "He'd suspect something."

He got back to pacing in all his glorious naked and ready glory, making a frustrated groan erupt from my chest. "Are you serious right now, Archer? You've been doing everything short of groveling at my feet to get me into bed, and now that I'm in it, you don't have any condoms?"

A pained look broke across his face when he took in the view of me lounging on his bed. "I didn't actually think you'd agree."

"So why all of the effort if you didn't think I'd eventually go against my better judgment and fall into bed with you?"

His eyes landed on mine from across the room. "Because I go after what I want, no matter the likelihood or, in your case, unlikelihood of it happening."

"Admirable. Even a little romantic." I tipped my head at him. "Except for your lack of planning and preparation." I motioned between him and me, an entire room keeping us apart thanks to one missing piece of latex.

Suddenly, Archer's face flattened like he was remembering something, and he bounded across the room. He pulled his wallet out of his coat pocket and shook it. Black shiny credit cards and large bills tumbled to the ground right before his face lit up. He pulled something from a small pocket.

"Fuck yes, I have one. I forgot all about it." His wallet dropped to the floor, his hand clutching the condom like it was a priceless artifact thrust into the air. A moment later, his forehead creased. "These things come with an expiration date though, right?" He lowered the condom so it was in front of his eyes, the skin between his brows creasing.

"Yeah," I said slowly. "So if you bought them in the Cretaceous Period, you might want to toss it out."

"Okay, no, we're good." His eyes squinted a little more as he read something on the wrapper. "At least for another month."

At the same time my body relaxed with relief knowing we'd be able to have sex soon, it tensed with nervousness at the same realization. "Why is the only condom Luke Archer has on him is about to expire?"

"It's been a while." The torn wrapper was already on the floor as he moved back toward the bed, the condom rolling into place down his hard length.

I had to swallow back the flames licking up my throat. “It’s been a while since what? You had to supply your own form of birth control?”

Archer stopped at the edge of the bed again, gently nudging my legs apart before stepping between them. “Since I’ve been with a woman.”

“How long?”

“A while.”

“In quantitative terms?” My eyes closed when he lowered his body over me, pressing my back into the mattress with his wide chest.

“I’d rather not confess that for fear of it ruining the mood,” he whispered then kissed my neck. “How long’s it been for you?”

Just feeling his naked body against mine, kissing me, my body ready to lose itself in the throes of pleasure, was enough of an answer to that question. “A while.”

Archer’s arm wound around me, sliding me back on the mattress until my head fell into the pillows. Every part of my body was connected to some part of his: our mouths as they explored each other again, our arms as he lifted mine above my head, his fingers knitting through mine and holding me there. The rest of our bodies were pressed together, wound together, moving together . . . Luke Archer was everywhere.

Everywhere but where I needed him to be right then.

When my hips tipped against him, pressing down when I felt him in place, he groaned against my mouth, shaking his head. “Not yet . . .” His tongue dove back into my mouth, stroking mine before his mouth left mine. "I make sure to hit every base before sliding into home plate."

I shook my head. "Still with the baseball references?"

I felt his smile curve against my mouth. "Always," he whispered, before his mouth moved lower. My breath caught in my throat when his mouth latched onto my nipple, sucking it. His tongue teased me, circling it a few times in such a way it made me wonder if I was going to orgasm from Luke Archer doing this and nothing more, before he released me.

"First base," he whispered, his tongue drawing a line across my chest before his lips formed around my other breast. This one he sucked harder, lashing it with his tongue until I was writhing below him in bed. He released it a minute later with a wet pop. "Second base."

When he glanced up at me beneath the frame of hair covering his forehead, the look in his eyes had a direct line to my sex. I moaned from that look, my head falling back on the pillows as his mouth trailed lower.

His tongue painted a wet line down my stomach, drawing every nerve I'd never known I had out of hibernation. Drawing every nerve to the surface of my skin where he was touching me.

My back arched as he traveled lower, and just when his tongue reached my belly button, his finger moved inside me. As his tongue circled my belly button a few times, his finger moved in and out, curling into me when it could go no deeper, and he found that spot that made me almost scream his name every time.

"I can't wait any longer. I'm sorry. I wanted to take my time, but fuck, I'm about to come right now, and there's no way we'll be twice lucky finding a condom." He kissed the sensitive area winding down my hip, pulling his finger out before crawling up my body. "I want to be inside you when I come. I need to be."

All I could do was nod, because I'd lost the capacity for speech one finger screwing ago.

At least I had right up until I saw his face form something of a wince when he made a sudden movement getting his legs between mine.

"You need to be careful," I said, still panting beneath him. I had to close my eyes to concentrate when I felt him move into position. "No leg movement. You need to keep the muscle stationary. In fact, I should be on top to make sure you listen."

Archer's arms fell into the pillows on either side of my head, pinning me beneath him. "Sorry. There is no way I'm going to just lay there during our first time."

When he tipped his hips into mine, starting to move inside me, my fingers dug into his back.

"Our second? Third? Maybe. But our first time, I want to be on top of you, my body pinning yours beneath mine, my face hovering above yours." His face moved right above mine then, his eyes unblinking. "I want to watch you as I make you come. I want you to watch me when you make me come. I want to watch everything so I know what makes your eyes close, what makes your mouth fall open, what makes your face flush. I want to know so I can give you everything you need. Whenever you need it."

He kissed my mouth sweetly then, right before driving the rest of himself inside me. My moan of pleasure tangled with his, filling the four walls of his hotel room. His mouth dropped outside of my ear as he started to move inside me, breathing hard as our bodies started spiraling together in their shared release.

"I want to know everything there is to know about you, Allie Eden."

chapter Eight

OUR FIRST TIME had been the best sex of my life. Our first time had also been the shortest sex of my life.

All it had taken was feeling him moving inside me a few times before my body lost control, the power of my orgasm bringing him to his own release. I'd never come so quickly. Ever. It was almost like Luke's body had been created to please mine as quickly and as powerfully as possible. It almost was like mine was had been built the same for him.

Sex with Luke Archer made me question what I'd been doing with men before, because whatever that had been, it wasn't the same. It wasn't even in the same galaxy.

The one downside to having that kind of sex was that I wanted to do it again. Right after.

But we were in a bit of a condom supply crisis.

When Luke had come out of the bathroom with a towel tied around his waist, he grabbed a twenty-dollar bill from the floor as he headed for the door to go in search of the missing contraband, and I'd barely managed to stop him.

At least I barely had until I dropped to my knees, my mouth wrapping around him. He collapsed into the door, his mission to find a box of rubbers long forgotten.

I'd never experienced or given so much oral in my life, but desperate times called for desperate measures, and Luke Archer's head between my legs wasn't exactly a poor substitute for his dick.

This round, he'd backed me into a wall, lifted me until my legs were tangled over his shoulders, and lowered his head between my legs.

"God, Luke," I moaned, my back bumping against the wall as he assaulted me with his mouth. "After this . . . you need another . . ."—my fingers raked through his hair as his tongue fluttered against me—"ice and heat treatment."

He murmured his answer against me, making my head fall back into the wall.

"Are you sure you don't want a muscle relaxer or . . ."—his finger sank into me, another one joining it—". . . or something?"

His mouth left me just long enough to answer. "My tongue's a muscle." Said muscle circled a very sensitive part of my body. "Are you sure you want my muscles relaxed?" Said tongue got back to lashing across me, drawing my orgasm from deep in my body.

"Scratch the muscle relaxers." I sighed, my hips riding his fingers still plunging in and out of me. "Just don't stop."

I could practically feel his smirk against me right before he sucked at my clit, and that was all it took. My body went rigid at the top of my orgasm right before thrusting my hips against him as he continued to work my body, not stopping until the last aftershocks of my release had long been finished.

"Good?" he said a minute later, leaving a trail of kisses down my inner thigh.

"Do you need an actual verbal confirmation?"

"I'm a guy. We like verbal confirmations."

Running my fingers through his hair, I smiled down at him, my chest still firing from my breathing. "Then that was so much better than good, there hasn't been a word created for what that was because so few people have experienced it."

He winked up at me. "Now that's a verbal confirmation.," he said, lifting me just enough to make untangling my shaking legs from his shoulders possible. Then he slowly slid me down the wall, maintaining his hold on me when my feet hit the floor, probably worried I'd collapse if he let go.

Which I might have.

"I still can't believe you almost came up empty in the condom department."

Luke's arms caged around my head, his head lowering until it was level with mine. "I wasn't exactly expecting last night."

"You weren't?" I raised a doubtful eyebrow at him.

"Hoping, always hoping." The corner of his mouth twitched. "But I didn't think I'd worn you down anywhere close enough for that."

"So I'm easier than I seem," I teased. "My parents would be proud."

He chuckled. "Thank god for that, because you had me worried we'd finally be doing it on my deathbed by the time you came around."

"Yeah, that condom hiding in your wallet definitely would have exceeded its shelf life by then."

"Although if you were ninety, I think your baby-making days would be over."

I made a clucking sound with my tongue, running my hands down his sides. His skin was warm, and a sheen of sweat clung to him. "Ah, the perks of geriatric sex. I mean, sure, you might break a hip, but you can ride bareback without worrying about knocking a grandma up."

Luke shook his head before kissing my forehead. "You're strange."

"Thank you," I replied, right before the alarm on my phone went off. "Time for your bath."

Luke groaned. "Can we just say we did and not?"

My hand dropped to his right leg, lightly curling around his inner thigh. The swelling had gone down some, but it was still inflamed. "Definitely not. You're lucky you didn't injure it worse with all of the *thrusting* you did last night. As it is, you're lucky I'm not putting you on a two-hour rotation instead of a three-hour." Ducking beneath the brace of his arms, I headed for my phone to turn off the alarm. It was seven in the morning, and the team was to head out from the hotel at nine. I had a lot to get done in two hours and, unfortunately, no time to *do* Luke anymore.

"I think your and my definitions of lucky are different."

Laughing, I paused just outside the bathroom door to admire him. He was still buttressed up against the wall he'd just gotten me off on. The morning sun coming through the window across from him bathed him in golden light, almost making him glow, highlighting a body that hinted at perfection. When his face turned toward me, my breath caught in my lungs. This man could not be real. That this man seemed into me and almost made for me could not be real either.

When his smile crept into place, I accepted that, real or not, I was going to let myself enjoy this time with Luke Archer. No matter how brief it was, no matter how careful we had to be, I was going to enjoy it because life didn't hand out an abundance of these kinds of experiences.

These were the kinds of memories people held onto instead of trying to forget.

"Thank you, Luke."

His head tipped. "For what?"

My answer was forming when a pounding sounded on the outside of the door.

"Room service," he said, snagging his sweats from the floor and sliding them into place.

"Good. I'm starving." Pulling one of the hotel robes from the closet, I slid into it.

"Can't imagine why." Luke smirked at me before pulling the door open.

"You are so lucky I'm not Coach right now." A voice I was not expecting broke into the room right before

Reynolds did. "Because heads would roll if he saw you upright, starting with yours."

Lunging the few steps into the bathroom, I shut the door and locked it. Reynolds hadn't seen me, but that had been close. So much for placing such a high priority on being careful.

I'd just have to hang out in here until he left, and we'd have to implement a check-the-peephole policy before opening the door for anyone when I was traipsing around Luke's hotel room, freshly fucked and wearing a bathrobe.

"Does Eden know you're up on your feet right now? Because I'd be more scared of her seeing you up than Coach."

Shit. It would seem strange if Reynolds didn't see me doing something that an athletic trainer who hadn't spent most of the night naked with the man she was tending to should be doing.

Thank god I'd stuffed my suitcase in here last night. I could step out of the bathroom in clothes instead of a plush white robe with the hotel's emblem and fine print that read *Archer and I Got It On Last Night.*

As I rustled through my suitcase, scrambling for a fresh set of clothes, I could make out Luke's and Reynolds's voices in the other room. It sounded like they were talking about the upcoming game, but there was a little too much adrenaline shooting through my system to focus on anything besides getting dressed before Reynolds got suspicious.

I'd guessed that if Luke and I kept this kind of relationship up for any kind of duration, someone would eventually figure it out—I hadn't guessed it would happen less than eight hours later.

Once I'd wrestled into the usual khakis and team polo I wore during the season, I flew to the bath and cranked on the water. There were a few bags of fresh ice piled on the floor, so I started upending them into the tub while it filled.

After a couple of minutes passed and I was reasonably certain I'd composed myself and would be up to the task of convincing Reynolds I'd done nothing more than perform my role of athletic trainer last night, I moved toward the door. Luke and Reynolds were still talking about the upcoming game when I pulled open the door.

"Hey, Doc." Reynolds's gaze immediately shifted my way as I stepped out of the bathroom. "Morning."

"Oh great." I crossed my arms and tried to ignore Luke watching me. Even just looking at me, he could fluster me. "You're calling me Doc now too?"

Reynolds shrugged. "Everyone is."

"Beautiful. Shepherd ought to love that," I muttered, casually scanning the floor to find that, somehow, Luke had managed to kick all evidence of an all-night sexathon under the bed. Except for . . .

Before my heart leapt into my throat, Luke moved toward the wrapper and discreetly stepped on it to hide it from view.

"Wow." Reynolds's forehead creased when he took a good look at me. "You look like he rode you hard and put you out wet. Forgive the analogy."

Luke was behind Reynolds, so he was free to laugh silently. I didn't have the same luxury.

"Forgiven," I said, moving toward my training bag to look busy. "And good for you for knowing what an analogy is."

"He didn't give you a hard time, did he? Archer can be a real hardass when he puts his mind to it."

My fingers fumbled with the zipper as I pulled the bag open. Luke continued to chuckle to himself across the room. "He gave me a pretty hard time."

"Dammit, Archer, I like this one." Reynolds lifted his middle finger at Luke. "We all like Doc. You mess this up and she leaves, my cleats are going up your ass."

"Is there a reason you're here? Other than to threaten to sodomize me with your size twelves?" Luke checked the clock, a pensive look casting over his face. I knew what he was thinking, but no, we did not have time for one more round.

"Yeah, I wanted to check on Doc. Make sure she survived the night with you."

"She survived the night. I think she might have even enjoyed herself a little." Luke's eyes flashed as he slowly licked his lips when Reyolds wasn't looking.

Ignoring the chills tumbling down my spine, I smiled at Reynolds. "Who wouldn't enjoy giving a guy like Archer six ice baths in one night, right?"

Reynolds snorted a laugh before tipping his chin at me, flipping Archer off again, and heading toward the door.

"Hey, Reynolds," Archer called as Reynolds was

pulling the door open, "would you mind if I borrowed . . ."—he jacked his brows at me a few times, my heart calcifying in my chest—"an extra pair of socks?"

My whole body sagged in relief. Right before I shot a glare Luke's way for nearly giving me a heart attack.

"Sure. No prob," Reynolds replied. "For a minute you had me worried there. I thought you were going to ask to borrow my jock or something."

"Oh no. Yours wouldn't fit me." Luke shook his head, glancing at his jock region. "I have to special order. They don't make them in my size."

Reynolds grunted. "Yeah, well, that's what you get for wearing too tight of briefs growing up. You stunted its growth."

Luke smirked at him. "Come on, Reynolds. You know I grew up by a nuclear reactor. Don't be a hater. Penis envy is a real and treatable disorder. There are professionals you can talk with about your feelings of inadequacy and impaired size."

Luke got the double bird that time. Reynolds left the room with a string of good-natured curses laced with comebacks.

My shoulders slumped when the door closed. "That was close."

Lifting his foot, Luke bent to grab the condom wrapper before tossing it in the wastebasket by the desk. "Yeah, sorry. I totally thought that was our breakfast."

"You don't think he suspects anything, do you?"

"About the real *hard* time I gave you last night?" His dimple set into his right cheek from his smile. "No. Reynolds is convinced the only game I have is what I exude on the field."

When the next knock pounded on the door, I lifted my finger when he lunged toward the door.

"But you're dressed now." He shrugged before his face lined. "Speaking of, why are you dressed? We've still got two hours before we have to be downstairs."

My eyes lifted. "Just check the peephole, please."

Luke shrugged but did as asked. A second later, his hands came together. "Breakfast."

My stomach rumbled at the promise of sustenance.

Once the employee had rolled the cart into the room and turned to go, Luke stopped him at the door. Even though he'd turned his back toward me as he riffled through his wallet, I didn't miss the tip Luke gave the employee. If I'd missed the bill, the look on the guy's face would have given it away.

"Breakfast didn't cost a quarter that much probably, you know that?"

"Do I know what?" Luke gave me an innocent look as he settled his wallet back on the dresser before rolling the breakfast cart toward the bed.

"How about the table?" I nodded at the table and chairs propped by the window. "I don't trust you to eat breakfast if you and I are on the same bed together."

Luke's mouth curved. "Breakfast in bed is my favorite way to dine."

My stomach muscles tightened. "Do you ever *not* have that on your mind?"

"When you're around?" Luke shook his head. "Never."

"Then breakfast at the table far away from the bed for sure. I can't have you malnourished in addition to injured."

Luke rolled the cart toward the table, his smirk amplifying. "Please. I was up all night eating. Malnourished I am not."

I should have been oversexed and exhausted, but at his words and his look, that very part of my body he was alluding to pulsed with desire.

In an attempt to ignore it, I started laying the breakfast trays on the table. "I was a little too preoccupied last night to notice, but why is Luke Archer in a standard room? The same kind of standard room the team puts grunt workers like myself in? I would have thought they'd put their prized possession in some suite complete with a bowling alley and a lap pool."

Luke poured two cups of coffee from the silver carafe, stirring milk and sugar into the cup in front of me. "I don't need a big room. I don't need a fancy suite with bowling alleys and lap pools and pinball machines. Or whatever the hell are in them. I just need a place to sleep before heading out for the next game." He mixed some sugar into his cup, then sat down across the table from me.

"So Luke Archer is low maintenance?"

His head shook. "Luke Archer is *no* maintenance. I mean, yeah, maybe one day if I'm still doing this when I have a family, then a bowling alley would be fun, but for now, it's just me. I don't need a whole lot."

"My experience with you last night leads me to another conclusion."

"Sex is different. Everyone needs a whole lot. I need a whole, *whole* lot. I thought we were talking about hotel rooms."

Fighting my smile, I lifted the metal cover from my plate to find pancakes, scrambled eggs, and bacon. The skin between my brows pinched together as I stared at the plate in front of me.

"Something wrong?" Luke asked as he took the cover off his plate.

Checking to see if he had the same thing, I discovered that no, he had a big omelet with a side of hash browns and toast. "Who ordered this?"

"I did." He shrugged, his tone hinting that it should have been obvious.

"Did you make a lucky guess or something?" When his brows stayed lifted, I circled my fork at my plate. "This is my favorite breakfast. What I almost always order when I'm on the road."

"Yeah, I know." Luke scooted the syrup toward me. "That's why I ordered it for you."

"How did you know that?" I moved past the initial shock to take a bite of my bacon.

"I told you, Allie. I noticed you from the first day you started. I haven't stopped noticing you either." Luke winked across the table at me. "Right down to what you like to eat every morning for breakfast."

I froze with the piece of bacon still in my hand. "You noticed that much about me? Right down to the way I like my eggs cooked and my pancakes butter free?"

He shrugged again, his face indicating that this all should be obvious. "Yeah." He lifted his coffee cup and drained it in one drink. "Someone in my position—someone in your position—can't just rush into something. You need to take your time. Observe someone from way back before coming closer. That's what I did with you." He watched me pour him another cup of coffee like I was proving some point he was trying to make. "I noticed how you were always at work before anyone else. How you were usually the last one to leave too. How you hustled everywhere you went, were the first on the field when a guy needed help, and didn't take crap from anyone. That told me everything I needed to know about your character. That you're hard-working, dedicated, and compassionate." He cut into his omelet with the side of his fork. "The rest, I'd figured out way before that."

"The rest?" I asked, pouring a stream of syrup over my pancakes. I added more than usual, hoping the extra sugar would make up for the lack of sleep.

"The attraction part," he said, waving his fork between us.

"Really? You were attracted to me that early on?"

The morning light streaming through the window caught his eyes, setting them on fire. "From the first time I saw you."

The bite of pancake froze outside my mouth. "Come on. Be serious."

"I am." He finished chewing the heap of omelet he'd just stuffed into his mouth. "Are you going to tell me you've never looked at a person and known you were attracted to them? You might not know their name or anything about them, but you do know that something inside you is drawn to something inside them?"

Shifting in my chair, I thought that over as I chewed on the best room service pancakes I'd ever had. Might have had something to do with what I'd been doing to work up my appetite for them. "I guess so."

"I felt that with you," he said, as matter-of-factly as if he were talking about batting averages or win ratios. "So I started paying closer attention to you. Everything seemed so perfect: the schedule, who you were. Everything was perfect except . . ." His head tipped from side to side. "You didn't seem to know I existed."

"You're Luke Archer. Believe me, I knew you existed."

"Well, you didn't act like it."

Making like Luke, I drained my first cup of coffee in one long drink. I was going to need the sugar and caffeine to get through today. "Well, you didn't act like I did either, so I guess we're equal."

Luke chuckled as he crunched on his toast. "Middle school courting at its finest. Pretending the person you're into doesn't exist."

"Well, look at us now." I glanced across the table at him. I was eating breakfast with a shirtless Luke Archer after experiencing a night of wild abandon and even wilder sex.

"Yeah, look at us now." He filled my cup of coffee back up and shot me a wink. "It's hard to beat a person who never gives up."

"Mr. Ruth?"

He nodded. "Mr. Ruth."

We were quiet for a minute, working on our breakfasts and enjoying the peaceful silence. I didn't feel the need to fill it. Luke didn't seem to feel the need either. We were comfortable with the quiet, which seemed like the highest step a couple could aspire to. Strange, since we'd only known each other for weeks and been "together" for hours.

I broke the silence once we were pushing the last few bites of our meals around. "So how are we going to make sure that no one finds out?"

"We'll have to be discreet," he said.

"Are you capable of being discreet?"

"I am when I have to be. When I've got the proper motivation."

"And this, us, is proper motivation?"

"This, us"—he waved his fork between us—"is the definition of proper motivation."

The dead serious look on his face made me laugh. Male motivation was not one of the great mysteries of life. "You've got a date with an ice bath, but I've got one more question before I give your family jewels frostbite."

"Good one."

I continued, "If you'd been watching me for a while—been attracted to me for a while—why did you decide that night on the plane was the right time to make your move?"

His eyes lifted to mine as he buttered his toast. "You're telling me my opening line of *whose ass do I need to kick, Doc* didn't do it for you?"

"It worked, obviously, but it was a unique approach."

Luke stretched his legs out and leaned back into his chair. "No, that hadn't been part of my plan at all, but seeing you sitting there, looking so sad, I didn't care. I had to talk to you."

Something inside me softened right then. Maybe it was my heart. Maybe it was my head. Maybe it was both. "You're kind of wonderful, Luke Archer."

He set his hand on the table, holding it open and waiting. When my hand settled into his, he held it tightly. "You're kind of wonderful too, Allie Eden."

chapter *Nine*

BEING DISCREET WAS harder to do than I'd guessed. Luke was actually doing better with it than I was. I kept finding myself checking the duration of my stares or the degree of my smiles or the tenor of my touch when I changed his compress. Second-guessing and self-regulating had become the way of things ever since we checked out of the hotel in Florida.

For all of the effort, I was confident we'd done a decent job of coming across as nothing more than one trainer and one player working together. A couple of raised brows from Reynolds that I wrote off as muscle spasms—Reynolds was the kind of guy who wouldn't notice much unless a couple was straight-up getting it on a foot in front of him—was all the suspicion I'd noticed aimed our way. Of course, once the *Sports Anonymous* cover came out, we'd see more.

We were in New Orleans, and it was a game day. After checking into the hotel last night, Luke and I had gone to our respective rooms, though not from his lack of trying to change that. But I was too worried about someone catching me slipping into his room or him sneaking out of mine. Without the excuse of round the clock treatment, there'd be no reason other than the obvious for a woman to be in Luke Archer's hotel room at night.

The team and staff had checked into the locker room an hour ago, and I'd been busy taping, massaging, and stretching the players. I hadn't seen Luke since he'd finished his ice bath a while ago, but I found my gaze shifting over to his designated locker, with his uniform and cleats, every few minutes, wondering where he was.

"Eden!" Coach Beckett's voice echoed through the entire locker room. "My office!" He didn't wait for me to acknowledge him or pause to locate me in the room—he just marched back into the coach's office.

"Thanks, Doc," Watson, one of the team's back-up pitchers, said, winding his arm a few times after I succinctly had to finish my massage.

"You bet. Just make sure you give yourself a proper warm-up tonight before you jump the mound and start throwing one hundred mile speedballs, okay? That's how you get on the list for needing a new shoulder before your thirtieth birthday."

Watson acknowledged me with a grunt as I headed for the coach's office. I didn't have a clue what Coach wanted to see me about, but it wasn't uncommon for us to have trainers' meetings with him if he needed to be brought up to speed on a player's status. Those were scheduled though, and never held a mere few hours before a big game.

When I stepped inside the office, I found I wasn't the only one Coach had rounded up. Shepherd; the team's doctor, Dr. Callahan; and Turner, the physical therapist, were all circled around someone sitting in a chair across from the coach's desk.

Luke.

He didn't divert his attention toward me when I entered the room; he kept his gaze on Coach and his expression conventional. He was in a pair of jeans, a snug-fitting white tee, and had his team ball cap on backward, sending the ends of his hair curling out around the rim of it.

Even being in a room packed with other bodies and neither of us really acknowledging each other, I had a difficult time staying unaffected. The air became a little thinner. My heartbeat a little louder. My breaths a little shorter.

"What do you have to say about this, Eden?" Coach stood behind the desk, already in his uniform and windbreaker, pointing straight at Luke.

My throat constricted at the same time the air rushed out of my lungs. All the eyes in the room, except for Luke's, turned on me, all of them waiting for my response. Had someone found out? Is that what this unscheduled meeting was about?

My mind went blank as the silence continued.

"Am I speaking in gibberish or something?" Coach grunted, staggering his hands across the desk as he leaned across it. "You've spent the last two days with Archer. Start talking."

My pulse felt like a drumbeat in my throat as adrenaline and anxiety flooded my system. Coach's stare was unyielding, and the longer I stayed quiet, scrambling for something to say, the more imaginary steam seemed to blow from his ears.

Shepherd's forehead was drawn together, appraising me with a look that indicated he thought me quite inept. Dr. Callahan's and Turner's expressions weren't that much better. Archer was the only one not looking at me, but as my silence stretched on, he shifted in his seat.

"My leg." His voice filled the room. "How do you think my leg's doing?"

When he let his head turn just enough in my direction so our eyes connected, I relaxed. This wasn't a meeting accusing Archer and me of having an inappropriate relationship—this was a status meeting about his leg.

My lungs went from two limp, sagging balloons to bursting. "It's a stage two pull, as you all know," I started, having to look away from Archer in order to speak intelligibly. "We continued to treat it through the night, alternating ice and heat, every three hours. The plan is to continue the same through tonight, start some massage and stretching tomorrow, and take it from there."

Coach was whirling his hand like he was waiting for me to say more. When I didn't add anything else, he threw his arms in Archer's direction. "Fantastic. But what does that have to do with tonight's game?"

"Tonight's game?" I felt my eyebrows pinch together as I glanced at Archer, still perfectly stoic-faced in his chair, almost like he was waiting to be read a sentence in court.

Coach grumbled something, his cleats clinking on the floor as he started pacing behind the desk. "Yes, can he play or not?" My eyebrows stayed together as he continued, "I've gotten everyone else's opinion on the matter, and now I'd like yours. If it wouldn't be too big of an inconvenience for you to give it, of course." Coach shot me a look.

I stood quietly confused for another moment. Waving at Archer, the only one sitting in the room, and ripe from ice and heat treatments, I felt like the answer should have been obvious. "No." My voice seemed to fill the whole room. "He can't play tonight."

I didn't miss the way Archer's jaw tightened, his eyes narrowing just enough to give away he wasn't as removed as he was letting on. I also didn't miss the rest of the bodies in the room shifting. Shepherd huffed under his breath as his head shook.

Coach didn't seem to notice any of it—he just kept watching me like he was challenging me to change my answer or something. I wouldn't though. With this kind of injury, playing a game less than forty-eight hours later shouldn't even be open to discussion. Archer was out for one game at least, if not a few. It was difficult to say for sure since with an injury like his, you had to take it day by day.

"I've got four other people in the room telling me the opposite, Eden." Coach paused his pacing, his hands going to his hips as he studied Archer in his chair. "What reason do you have to give me for why my star player can't play a big game tonight?"

Three sets of eyes slid in my direction, varying degrees of smugness and superiority on Shepherd's, Callahan's, and Turner's faces. I returned their looks with one of my own. They all damn well knew it wasn't in Archer's best interest to return to the game tonight. Maybe it was in the team's, but it wasn't for the player.

"Ignoring the fact that he could barely walk unassisted yesterday," I began, peaking my brow, "if you put him in the game tonight, Archer has a very high likelihood of reinjuring himself—and much worse. Then your star player might have to sit out the rest of the season instead of a couple of games."

Coach let that process for a minute while I crossed my arms at the three other people in the room who should have been on board with me. I couldn't believe that a damn doctor, physical therapist, and the lead athletic trainer would look Coach in the eye and tell him Archer could play tonight.

It was the training profession's equivalent of malpractice.

But Coach had said the four people in the room had told him Archer could play tonight which meant . . .

My head whipped in Archer's direction when I put it together. I'd told him he couldn't play tonight. I'd prepared him because I knew he wouldn't take sitting out a game well. I couldn't believe he'd hear me tell him one thing, then go on to tell Coach something else. Anger surged in my veins, and my stare progressed to the point of almost willing him to look at me.

He wouldn't though. His jaw stayed locked as his stare seemed capable of almost melting the wall in front of him.

"Archer?" Coach's voice boomed in the room. "You're sitting out tonight."

Three annoyed sighs sounded through the room, but all Archer did was give a small tip of his head in acknowledgment.

"We'll reconvene before the next game, but you'd better make sure you're listening to the medical team and getting this leg fixed. No more of this tough guy shit, Archer. This team needs you, and not in the form of you riding the bench, you hear me?"

Archer lifted his gaze to Coach's, his hands gripping the armrests of the chair. "Understood." Then he shoved out of his chair and left the room without so much as a sideways look in my direction.

chapter *Ten*

WE'D LOST. BY a run.

A few of my colleagues who had been in Coach's office earlier made no attempts to dull their pointed looks of blame my way. Yes, the Shock may very well have won if Archer had been playing, but they also could have been looking at losing a hell of a lot more had he played and injured himself worse.

I shouldn't feel guilty—I'd made the right call—but I couldn't fight the sliver of it I felt. Of course second-guessing came into play too, making me question if I should have said something to Coach about the way Archer had been favoring his leg during those last few innings of the game against the Rays. But if I had and Archer had been benched the last few innings, he wouldn't have been able to make a hit that brought in two runs in the ninth and won the Shock the game.

Second-guessing was part of the job. It was part of life. I tried to make the best decisions I could and not let myself get hung up in the what-ifs. Which was harder to do when it came to Luke Archer than with anything else in my life.

Even though he'd ridden the bench the whole game, cheering his teammates from the dugout, we hadn't exchanged more than a few clipped words and bags of ice. I told myself that this was the way we'd have to act around each other when we were with the team, but it still felt odd when the man I'd slept with two nights ago wouldn't make eye contact when I held out a fresh bottle of water for him.

Whether or not this was part of his act to keep our relationship—whatever it was exactly—hidden, I knew one thing for sure—he was angry. I hadn't sided with him and the rest of the Lip Service Crew, and as a result, he'd had to sit out a game. In his entire professional career, Luke Archer had never sat out a game. Knowing who he was, I guessed that was how he had been planning on retiring from his career.

So he was upset at me for making the right call. That was fine. I could handle a player pouting because I had to tell him he wasn't immortal and that mortal instruments like flesh and blood were vulnerable. The more time I'd had to think about it, the madder I'd gotten over the whole thing.

Who was he to get all upset at me for making a good, honest call? I'd only been doing my job, and I'd do it again if I felt it was in his best interest to sit out a game. I didn't care who he was or how he made me feel—my job came first. It had to. It was all I could count on at the end of the season, because I wasn't sure Archer would still be there. I might have hoped he would be, but I wasn't a total fool. A relationship as new as ours, as forbidden as ours . . . the probability of it enduring wasn't on the promising end of the scale.

Since my thoughts had been a bit flustered, I paused to study the wrap I'd just finished on Reynolds's ankle. "Is that too tight?" I asked, testing beneath the bandage with my finger to make sure I wasn't cutting off the circulation to his foot.

"Nothing could ever be too tight, Doc." Reynolds was no doubt grinning down at me with his brows in his hairline.

"You might change your mind if your toes fall off from lack of blood flow." I tested the wrap on the other side to find it was okay. Reynolds's toes would live to see another day.

It was a little after the game, and the Shock were dotted around the locker room, not making their usual post-game noises and chest bumps. The mood was somber, if not downright depressing. The sound of the showers and the squeak of locker hinges were about all of the noise spilling about the room.

Well, and of course Reynolds's unending soliloquy of innuendos.

"While you're down there, Doc . . ." Reynolds bobbed those raised brows when I looked up at him with a sigh.

"Watch your mouth, Reynolds." A looming frame towered up behind me.

I didn't need to turn around to know who it was. The

tone of his voice might have been unfamiliar, but the way my body responded when his came near was not.

Reynolds's face creased. "Whoa. Ease up there, Archer." He lifted his hands. "I meant no disrespect. Sorry."

I pretended to still be busy testing the bandage to keep distracted.

"It's not me you owe an apology to."

Reynolds continued to study Archer like he was confused, which he had every right to be. Archer was known for being laid-back and easygoing. There was nothing laid-back or easygoing about his tone or words.

"Sorry, Doc," Reynolds said as I stood. "I was just being my usual asshole self. I didn't mean anything by it."

"I know you didn't," I enunciated slowly, more for the man behind me than the one in front of me. "Forget about it."

Reynolds looked at Archer, his shrug reading *we good?*

"Watch your mouth. For once." Archer passed me without a look, heading for the showers.

"Dude, I didn't know Archer could be pissy. I didn't think he had it in him."

"He's not mad at you. He's mad at me for telling Coach he should sit the game out." I nudged Reynolds.

"Plus you've been icing the shit out of his balls, Doc. A man can only take so much of that torture." Reynolds's hand went to his crotch, like he was protecting his own balls from getting iced by me.

"Thanks for the tip. I'll keep that in mind."

Reynolds fired a salute before starting to tear out of his jersey while I moved onto the next player on my list.

After that, the locker room cleared out faster than normal. It probably had to do with the guys not being in the mood to celebrate. I was in one of the back rooms, re-stocking my bag with the supplies I'd run through during tonight's game, when I heard a pair of cleats echo inside the room.

"You are still here, good. Should have figured." Coach Beckett was still in his jersey and cleats. In fact, I wasn't sure anyone had ever not seen him in his jersey and cleats, which had led to the rumor that the man slept in them.

"What can I do for you, Coach?" I asked, stuffing a few more rolls of athletic tape into my bag.

"I just wanted to say thanks for giving it to me straight earlier about Archer. I appreciate that. In fact, I need that. Too many of these people are just going to tell me whatever they think I want to hear, but I need someone who's going to tell me what I *need* to hear." Coach crossed his arms and tipped his head. "I hate losing a game, but what I hate more is losing a season. Good job tonight, Eden." Before I could say anything, he turned to leave. "The team bus already headed out to the hotel, but there'll be a car waiting for you and Archer when you're ready to leave."

My hands froze inside my bag. "Archer's still here?"

"Yep. Just you two left." His voice echoed as he moved through the locker room.

I waited inside the backroom for a few minutes,

thinking. I wanted to talk to him, but I wasn't sure if he felt the same.

Stalling for a few more minutes, I decided to go find him. I hadn't gotten where I had by being timid and complacent. I wouldn't approach whatever this was between Archer and me like that either.

Heading into the main part of the locker room, I found it dark and empty. All of the lockers had been cleaned out except for one. Number eleven's. He was nowhere in sight, but then I noticed the sound of the shower. If he was still in the shower room, he was about to qualify for the longest shower ever.

Then again, maybe someone had just forgotten to turn off one of the showers. I broke to a stop when I got inside the shower room. Someone had left a shower on, but that someone was still hovering beneath it, his head and arms pressed into the tile wall below the showerhead. Archer wasn't moving; he was just standing there, letting the water rain down on his back and spill down his body.

My throat ran dry watching him like this: naked, braced against the wall, water rolling down him, steam fogging around him. I had to remind myself I was mad at him because damn, there was nothing infuriating about the man stationed in front of me right now.

I felt other things, but anger wasn't part of the spectrum.

"Archer?"

He didn't respond. He didn't move.

"Is this how we're going to deal with this stuff when it comes up?" I took a few more steps inside the big shower room. "Giving each other the silent treatment?"

I waited a minute. Then two. I was about to turn and leave when he shifted.

"I could have played." His voice was low, guarded, but at least he was communicating.

"Yeah, you probably could have."

His head tipped over his shoulder. "Then why didn't you say that earlier?"

Crossing my arms, I moved closer. "Because I didn't think you *should* play."

A sharp exhale rolled out of his mouth. "I'm a ball player. I get paid to play. My job is to swing the bat and play the field. It isn't to ride the bench with a bag of ice between my legs."

"And I'm an athletic trainer. I get paid to take care of the players. My job is to prevent and treat injuries. It isn't to tell the coaching staff whatever they want to hear." I didn't stop moving until I'd reached the wall he was leaning into. Still keeping him at a distance, I turned so I was facing him.

"I've got a job to do." When his head turned toward me, his eyes found mine.

My hands lifted. "So do I, Luke. My job is to make sure you can continue to do yours. So back off." My voice was growing, bouncing off the walls of the shower room. "If you want someone who will tell you what you want to hear, Shepherd's really good at that."

His brows came together as he inspected me. "You're mad at me?" He sounded incredulous—he almost looked it too.

I gave him the same look right back. "Yeah, I tend to get a little touchy when people question my calls."

"Good." He shoved off the wall, turning to face me. Having the full view of him a few feet in front of me made me feel something I shouldn't have been experiencing in a locker room with a man I was upset with. "I'm kind of angry too."

"How is that good?"

A fire ignited in his eyes. "You're about to find out."

"Luke . . ." I warned, checking the entrance to the shower room.

This was too risky; I didn't care what Coach had said about us being the last two here. All it took was one of the players realizing he'd forgotten something and popping back in. Or one of the stadium janitorial staff coming in thinking the visiting team had all left. Luke Archer wasn't just some guy—he was arguably the best player in the sport. If anyone found out we'd done what I could tell he had in mind, the headlines would haunt me until the day I died.

"So I'm done talking with Doc now." His voice was low still, but this time, it was from desire instead of anger. "I want to talk with Allie."

When my eyes dropped from his, my theory about what he had in mind was confirmed. "You *are* talking to Allie."

"Just making sure." Going from frozen to a flash of heat, Archer grabbed me by the waist and pulled me in front of him. He shoved my back into the wet tile wall, pressing his body into mine to hold me there. "Hi."

His hands slipped around my waist as his mouth lowered to my neck. So much for being upset at me for benching him. Not that I was exactly upset at him for challenging my call anymore either. Not with the way he was ever so gently flexing his hips into mine, managing to stroke me with his erection through my pants.

"I missed you," he said.

"I thought you wanted to *talk* with Allie." My words seemed to echo off the tile walls as he continued to suck at my neck. "I don't think what you have in mind is talking."

I felt his smile curve against my skin. "It starts with talking. Talking can even be interspersed throughout." He tugged my shirt out of my pants, his hands instantly sliding up the plane of my stomach until they were molding around my chest. He pried my bra cups down to expose my nipples, and his fingers explored them until I could feel my heartbeat pulsing between my legs.

"What are you doing, Luke?"

Nipping at the skin stretching across my collarbone, he leaned back just enough to rip my shirt over my head. He threw it down the row of showers. "Getting ready to fuck you up against this tile wall. What do you think I've been doing in here all night?"

My thighs squeezed together. "Waiting for me?"

His hands returned to my chest, the look on his face intent. "Waiting to be inside you."

"I thought you were avoiding me."

"No, I definitely wasn't avoiding you. I was biding my time for you." His grip tightened around my breasts, his hips sliding me down the wall until I was directly beneath the shower stream. I was already damp from before, but it only took a few seconds for the rest of my body and clothes to get soaked.

"Why does sex tend to start with you getting me wet?" I asked, blinking shower water from my eyes.

The corner of his mouth twitched. "Because I like you wet. I like making you wet. Everywhere."

When he flexed his hips against me this time, my head fell back. After the never-ending night of sex we'd had two nights ago, and having to go without him last night, my body was quivering from withdrawal. I'd never felt this kind of desire before. This kind of desperation that clouded all degree of reason and resolve.

In this moment, all that mattered was Luke Archer's body and mine connecting in every way two bodies could connect. I was a one-track-minded organism who would do anything to get her fix.

"I need you, Allie." His fingers pulled the button of my khakis free, his finger plunging inside my panties before the zipper was down. "Can I have you? Can I use your body to get what I need?"

My fists curled against the tile wall when his finger circled me a few times.

"Yes," I breathed, "if I can use yours for the same."

Something vibrated low in Luke's chest when his finger slid lower, feeling my invitation on his fingers. "You can use me, have me, take me however you need to. Whenever you need to."

His hands moved to my hips, then I was spinning around, my bare chest spreading against the hard tile wall as he ripped my pants and underwear down my body.

When his hands returned to my hips, he pitched them back so my butt was arched up toward him. His finger moved to my opening, another rumble coming from his chest when he felt how ready I was for his body. "I want to ride you hard, Allie. I need it rough." His mouth moved outside of my ear as I felt him starting to stretch me open. "Is that okay?"

I answered him by rolling my hips, trying to take him all, but for the moment, he was restraining himself. He wouldn't let me have him until I'd answered.

"Yes," I breathed, almost panting from the sensation of his thick girth opening me.

As the shower rained down on my back and legs, Luke Archer about to bury himself inside me, I realized how much power this man already had over me. Never had I been anywhere close to letting a flame fuck me in some semi-public shower, exchanging filthy pleasantries like it came naturally. Never had I felt such a pull toward a man, making me not care about the consequences—at least, not when we were like this. All of those years of school and all of the hard work to get here and stay here . . . all of that was overshadowed by Luke Archer and the way he made my head and body feel.

"I want to take you bare. I'll pull out, but I need to feel your body against my body right now." When he pushed inside me a little more, my moan echoed off the tile walls.

"You forgot to get condoms again, didn't you?" I said, once I was able to form words again.

His fingers dug into my hips. "I didn't forget. I just don't want to use one right now." He sank a little deeper, his moan tangling with mine. "I'll pull out, I promise."

I cried in agony when he stopped moving deeper. I'd already told him I was on the shot, and we were both free and clear to have unprotected sex without fear of passing on anything unwanted. What was his big hang-up with wanting to be so careful?

"Archer," I breathed, my legs trembling, "enough talk already."

For one more moment, he was still, then he ground into me until I felt my ass sitting on his lap. My cry of pleasure filled the room, eclipsing the new sounds of our bodies moving against each other.

"How's that for enough talking?" Luke grunted behind me as he took me exactly as promised. "You like that?"

My head bobbed against the tile wall, my tits slapping the wet wall every time he hammered into me.

"As damn good as this feels, I cannot wait to pull out of you and coat your body with my release." Archer leaned over me, his arms pinning mine to the wall above my head as he continued to rut into me with quick, deep strokes. "I want to mark you as mine. Everywhere. Anywhere. Every day. Every night. I want part of me on or in some part of you every fucking minute of every fucking day." He nipped at my neck, making me jolt.

My fingers curled into my palms as my release unfurled from deep within. I could feel Luke was on the cusp of his own from the way the breath hissed from his mouth, his strokes slowing in speed but becoming more urgent.

"You drive me mad, Allie. In every single way a woman can drive a man mad." Releasing my hands, he pulled out of me right when I was on top of my orgasm. My cries of frustration didn't go unnoticed. His fingers slipped inside me, fucking me hard the way his dick just had been, as I heard him working himself over with his other hand. "Where do you want me?"

His fingers were bringing me close again, sending me down that never-ending spiral of pleasure. "Back there. I want to feel you all over my ass."

As he let out a drawn-out groan, I felt the warmth of his release spray across my backside, sending me over the edge of my own orgasm.

Crying his name, I rode his fingers like I'd rode his dick, desperate for the feeling of oneness and wholeness I felt when he was buried inside me. The sensation of his orgasm, warm and sticky on my backside, made my own that much more powerful.

"Damn, Allie. Feeling that tight little body of yours strangle the shit out of my fingers is hot as hell." He kept pumping his fingers in me, not stopping, only slowing, once my body collapsed in a spent heap between the support of his body and the shower wall.

I felt the result of our love making rolling down my thighs and ass, the warmth of the shower soothing my tired muscles.

"Allie?" Luke's voice was soft and sweet as he slid a sheet of my wet hair from my neck so he could kiss it.

"Hmm?" was all I could respond with.

His large arm wound around my body, cradling me to him. “You can get mad at me whenever you want.”

chapter Eleven

THE SUN DIDN'T beat me up the next morning. Actually, it was rare when that happened, especially during the season, when there weren't enough hours in the day to get the job done.

When I opened my hotel door to see about scrounging up some breakfast, I found a surprise waiting for me. Leaning into the wall directly across from my room, Luke stood with his hands stuffed in his pockets, the look on his face making it seem like he'd been expecting me right at that moment.

"Morning." His mouth pulled into a smile when he saw me.

"Early riser too?" I said, trying to hide my surprise that Luke Archer was standing outside my hotel door at five in the morning.

"Yep. Sleep and I don't really get along."

"How long have you been waiting here?" I glanced up and down the hall, just to make sure no one was watching. Luke's room was on a different floor, and he had no reason to be waiting for me outside my bedroom door . . . except for the reason we were both trying to keep secret.

"Only ten, fifteen minutes, I think." Luke lifted his wrist to check his watch. "Or a half hour. I don't know."

"You've been waiting here that long?"

His head tipped. "There wouldn't be any wait that was too long for you."

It was too early in the morning for my heart to be firing like this, but keeping it steady when Luke Archer was looking at me the way he was now was impossible.

"Next time you can just knock, okay? I've been up for a while."

"I didn't want to knock," he said, shaking his head. "If you invited me into your room, I didn't trust that my plan for this morning would go according to plan."

"That's implying I would have invited you into my room"—my brow lifted at him—"and what plan for this morning?"

"I want to take you on a date."

"A date." From my voice, one would think that was a foreign concept to me. "It's five o'clock in the morning."

"It's a breakfast date." Archer swept his arm down the hall toward the elevators, but I stayed where I was.

"Where is this breakfast date taking place?"

"The restaurant downstairs has your favorite breakfast, and not only that, they have hubcapped-sized pancakes. Sounds like your kind of place."

When the door a couple down opened, I came close to jumping out of my sneakers. It was just a guy in a suit holding a briefcase though. Archer turned his hat around so the bill was riding low on his face and lowered his head a little as the guy passed.

The businessman didn't seem to notice Luke—instead his eyes were fixed on me as he wandered by. "Good morning."

I greeted him back as he passed, almost missing the backward look he gave me. Archer, however, did not miss it. His eyes narrowed at the man's back until he'd disappeared into an elevator.

"What are you doing?" I asked as his narrowed eyes lingered on the elevator doors the man had disappeared behind.

"Holding back."

"Holding back from what?"

His gaze slowly drifted back to me. As his eyes scanned me, it seemed the man was already forgotten. "From lots of things." Shoving off the wall, he cleared his throat. "Ready?"

I took a moment to catch up. A lot was coming at me at 5:03 in the morning. Luke Archer wanted to take me on a date. A breakfast one. I'd never been on a breakfast date. Certainly never as a first date. With a professional baseball player. That player being on the same team I'd just landed my dream job on. The same player who'd given me the best sex of my life by an infinite margin but brought feelings to the surface that scared me. Feelings that ran deeper than I was used to. Feelings that felt too intense for the brevity of our relationship.

"The rest of the team is staying at this hotel, Luke.

Someone could see us on our 'date.'" Even as I voiced my concern, I fell into step beside him as he moved for the elevators.

"And all it would look like is an athletic trainer and a player who have been working together a lot lately having breakfast together. The only people who will know we're on a date are the two of us." He punched the down button and turned to face me. He was in a good-fitting pair of jeans, a thermal that clung to him in all the right places, and had on his team hat. He wasn't naked—he wasn't touching me—but my heartbeat didn't seem to know the difference.

"And you'll keep your hands, and other parts, to yourself?"

"If I have to," he answered as we stepped onto the elevator.

It was empty, and that wasn't good. Not when the doors were going to seal us shut inside a small space. I backed into the corner to put some space between us. When Luke noticed, a smirk started moving into place. Then he put himself in the opposite corner like he was proving something.

"Why a date?" I asked, cursing the elevator as it seemed to crawl down floors. "After everything we've already done . . ." I had to clear my throat when it felt like Luke was doing it to me all over again with that look. "It isn't like you have to woo me or anything. We kind of plowed through the normal steps of relationship progression."

A goofy grin spread on his face when I said plow.

"And what if I want to 'woo' you?"

"And what if I'm not the kind of girl who wants to be wooed?"

"You don't have to be into jewelry and movie dates to be wooed. You're special. I want to show you that. I want to prove that to you."

My body started to creep away from its corner. "I'm not the jewelry and movie dates type of girl."

"I know." He nodded. "You're the hubcapped-sized pancake type of girl. The one who'd rather have a tree planted than a dozen long-stemmed roses. The one who'd rather go boogie-boarding in Big Sur than have a spa day." He shoved out of his corner, moving toward me. "Need me to keep going?"

I bit my lip, shaking my head.

"Plus, I want to prove to you that I'm capable of doing more than the physical part of a relationship. As damn insanely perfect as you and I are in that department, I want to prove to you I'm available for the other stuff. That I'm open and capable of it."

The elevator doors couldn't have opened at a better time. The last of the air had been sucked out of the small space, and I was one more word or look away from throwing myself at him. The rush of fresh air washed over me, clearing my head as I stepped into the lobby on the first floor.

Other than the hotel employees, no one else was around, and the restaurant he led me to was the one only a few steps away from the elevators. He had actually given this more thought than just taking me to breakfast—he'd made sure it would be quiet and we wouldn't have to go far—and something about seeing that he'd put so much thought into this made me feel exactly what he'd promised to prove to me—that I was special to him.

The hostess clearly recognized Archer when we stepped inside the restaurant, but she must have been warned the Shock was in the building for the night and advised not to fangirl. She cleared her throat and diverted her gaze. "Two for breakfast?"

Luke's shoulder bumped mine. "Two for breakfast. And would it be okay if we had a table that's a little more private?"

The hostess fumbled with the menus, her cheeks going redder and redder with every word from him. The poor thing couldn't have been much out of high school. "Of course, Mr. Archer," she replied before she winced. "I mean, of course, *sir.* I have no idea what your name is."

By this point, I was starting to feel uncomfortable for her, especially when the menus slid out of her arms again as she led us to one of the tables tucked away from the open part of the dining room. There were only a couple diners in the restaurant and, thank god, none of them were from the Shock.

Once we'd slid into our booth—I'd had to eye the bench across from me when Luke started to slide in beside me—the hostess handed us our menus with shaky hands. "I'll take your order whenever you're ready." Her voice was just as shaky.

"We're ready now." Luke set the menu down and leaned across the table a little. "Do you mind if I order for you?" he whispered. "Because some girls really hate that, and you seem like one of those who might not be so into it."

I sighed to myself. I was sure this star-struck girl was harmless, but most people were not. If he really did mean to keep us a secret, he was going to have to figure out that he couldn't ask me those types of questions with those types of looks when others were around.

"I don't mind if you order for me *this* time. As long as you get my order right." I set my menu down and motioned at him to proceed.

The hostess couldn't make eye contact with Luke as he ordered. "We'd like two coffees with milk and sugar. She'd like the hubcap pancakes with a side of scrambled eggs and bacon." Luke jacked his brows at me like he was waiting for me to congratulate him or something for getting my order right. "And I'll have the southwest omelet with hash browns and wheat toast."

As soon as she finished writing down our orders, she bolted away, forgetting to collect the menus.

"Creature of habit too?" I asked, noticing he'd had the same thing for breakfast two mornings ago.

"When you find something you love and that works, why switch it up?"

"See? You get it. Everyone else says it's boring, but knowing what you love isn't boring. It's a sign of maturity and not being afraid to commit. All of those people who are always into trying new things are the ones I don't get. It's like holding a sign that says 'I don't know what I like or what I want because I don't know who I am.'" When I finally came up for air, I realized I'd just given him an earful at the crack of dawn. "Sorry."

He waved it off, looking amused. "Personal soapbox?"

"Something like that," I muttered, relieved when our coffees showed up.

The hostess's hands were still shaking, which was dangerous when she was holding two cups of coffee balanced on saucers, so I took each cup from her and set it down. She threw me a relieved look before dropping the sugar caddy and milk ramekin between us and dashing back to the kitchen.

"You're a thoughtful person," Archer said, taking the sugar packet I held out for him.

"I just didn't want to have to worry about treating heat blisters on your body in addition to what I already have to treat."

Archer chuckled as he stirred the sugar into his coffee. "So tell me about Allie Eden pre athletic trainer extraordinaire." He must have noticed the flash of panic that hit my face. "Not the exhaustive biography, just the Cliff's Notes. For now, at least."

Fixing my coffee, I stalled. How did one sum up their life in a few sentences? "I don't know, I grew up in a small town in Indiana, got my undergrad from Michigan State, and my graduate degree from UCLA. That's about it."

Luke tilted his head, mild amusement settling on his face. "Your family?"

"Oh," I swallowed, taking a drink of coffee. "My dad and mom still live back in Indiana. They got divorced when I was little, so I was shuffled around from house to house. I go home every once in a while, maybe at Thanksgiving or Christmas to visit."

"Do they ever come visit you at your home?" he asked.

I shook my head. "Flying to California is like flying to Mongolia to them. And the apartment I have back in California is not what I'd call 'my home.' It's more of a dwelling than anything."

He clasped his hands together, watching me. "Siblings?"

Another head shake. "Only child."

"That must have been lonely."

"It wasn't so much that. It was more feeling like I never had anywhere to call home, you know? I never felt like I had a place where I just knew it was home." I shrugged, trying to play it off, but really, I'd never felt like I had a home my whole life. I went from being a child passed from house to house, to a student changing from dorm to dorm, to a woman moving from apartment to apartment.

He watched me for a minute. Just as it looked as though he were about to say something, his phone rang in his pocket.

"Sorry, I thought I'd turned it off," he said, pulling it out to check the screen.

It wasn't like I was trying to look, but I didn't miss the name flashing on it—Alexis. I got back to making my coffee, feeling ridiculous for the tinge of jealousy settling into my stomach as I accepted that Luke Archer had had other women in his life before me.

"It's my sister," he said.

And just when I thought I couldn't feel any more ridiculous . . .

"Go ahead and take it," I said.

"You sure? This is a date—our first date—and what kind of date am I if I answer my phone on it?"

"The kind of guy who's a good big brother." I pointed my spoon at the phone buzzing in his hand. "Take it."

"Thanks," he said quickly before answering it. "Morning, sunshine . . . wait, it's three a.m. there—what are you doing up?" His smile dimmed instantly. "Hey, Alex, it's okay. Just take a breath. What is it?"

Maybe I should have pretended to look out the window or pull my own phone out to check emails, but since he hadn't stood and walked away to have some privacy, I figured he didn't mind if I overheard him.

Whatever his sister was saying made his jaw set.

"I never liked that guy to begin with. I didn't like the way he looked at you. I didn't like the way he'd leave you waiting to pick you up. I didn't like the way he treated you period."

Luke must have been cut off because he looked like he was all set to keep going. Instead, he shifted on the bench, his hand gripping his phone tightly enough it looked capable of crushing it.

"He did what?" Luke's palm pounded the table, making our cups rattle. He mouthed a quick *sorry* at me. "I want his number, Alex. Give me his number, because I'm going to call him and have a little chat about ways to treat a girl and ways not to treat a girl. And then I'm going to tell him what I'm going to do to him for hurting my little sister—"

I had to purse my lips to keep from smiling because it was clear just how pissed off Luke was, but watching this grown man about to pummel some kid for hurting his little sister was possibly the sweetest thing I'd ever witnessed.

"Fine, fine. You're right, I'll relax. This way I can come up with a plan that will inflict maximum pain for minimum jail time." Whatever his sister fired back made Luke chuckle. "Yeah, well, it's like what I told you all. No one messes with my sisters, and if they do, they better make their peace with god."

Luke took a drink of his coffee while his sister talked. I couldn't hear what she was saying, but she was saying a lot.

"What can I do? Name it. Anything." He was quiet for a moment, but it sounded like she was too. His fingers snapped. "I know. How about if all of you girls fly out to my game next weekend in San Diego? We'll hit the beach, down as much ice cream as we can eat, and I'll take you all shopping."

There wasn't silence on the other end anymore. There was squealing. From what sounded like multiple voices. Luke had to pull the phone back from his ear a ways.

"Let Anne know about the plan, and I'll work out the details with her." He paused until the shrieking had dialed down a few notches. "And don't forget, kiddo, no guy is worth giving up your dreams. If you learn nothing else from me, remember that. Don't let anyone take your dreams from you." His eyes met mine—there was something purposeful in them. "What am I doing? I'm on a date." Luke shrugged. "Yes, at five o'clock in the morning. Is there some dating rulebook I'm not aware of?"

Whatever his sister said made him roll his eyes. "No, not with anyone you know."

Pause.

"Yes, with someone I like. Someone who's sitting right across the table from me, hearing every word of this phone call."

Another pause.

"Because you called. When have I ever *not* answered when one of you have called?" It sounded like he was getting an earful for a minute, then he sighed. "Yes, I promise to try not to mess this up—" He must have been interrupted. "Alexis . . ." His jaw set. "Thank you for the sisterly advice. Now if you don't have any other boys who need a beating . . ."

I didn't miss what she said. *Not at present. I love you.*

"I love you too. Tell your sisters I love them and I'll check in with them after school." Ending the call, he slid the silencer on before stuffing his phone back in his pocket. "Sorry about that. Great way to kick off a first date, right?"

"I didn't mind a bit. Boy problems?"

Luke exhaled. "Always. It's kind of the norm when I have three little sisters in their teens."

I wrapped my hands around my coffee cup, debating my next question. Just because I didn't know all things Luke Archer didn't mean I hadn't heard some things.

"You're their guardian now?"

If he felt conflicted about what my question was alluding to, he didn't express it. "Guardian, mother, father, big brother, pretty much all of it." He stared into his coffee cup, contemplation creeping into his expression. "Anne has been our saving grace though. She's an old friend of the family, but now she's kind of like a live-in nanny. However, if I call her that in front of the girls, they give me 'the look.'"

"The look?"

"You know, The Look." He waited for me to process that. "The one the female species has created to turn specimens of the male species into piles of ash. The Look."

"Oh yes, that one," I said, playing along.

Archer grinned, spinning his coffee cup in his hands. "Anyway, Anne takes care of everything when I'm on the road during the season, and I do my best to fit in visits during home games and occasionally fly them all out to an away game."

"And take them shopping and out for junk food. The hardships."

He chuckled a couple of notes before his expression became serious. "You know what happened to my parents?"

Inhaling slowly, I nodded. "Only what I read in the papers a few years ago."

I might not have known much about Luke Archer's life before a week ago, but I did know about his parents being carjacked and murdered on their way home from celebrating their twenty-fifth wedding anniversary. The whole nation knew that story as that had happened right when Archer's career was taking off. The media ate it up, printing headlines about The Slayed Parents of Luke Archer. Sensationalizing the whole tragedy by highlighting facts of that night that should have been respected and left alone. Details about how Mr. Archer had shielded his wife with his body while an entire magazine had been emptied into them. Or how their wedding bands had been ripped off their dead bodies. Or how their hands were found tangled together, even in death.

The media had bled that story dry, and I'd guessed it was part of the reason Archer had seemed as closed off as he had. At least as he had at first, because now he didn't seem closed off at all.

Luke continued to stare into his coffee like he was seeing something in it no one else could see. "The girls were only ten, twelve, and fourteen at the time. We had family they could have gone to, but it would have meant relocating from Oceanside, and I wanted to keep as much normalcy in their lives as possible. I wanted them to stay at the same school, with the same friends, in the same activities, you know?" His forehead creased deeper for a moment, then his whole face cleared. Like he'd just come from the dark into the light.

Lifting his cup, he took a drink of his coffee. "I applied for guardianship, and we've done our best to put the pieces back together. That's part of the reason my career is so important to me. I'm responsible for three human beings, and I want them to have any door they want open to them. I want them to be able to go to the best school in the country if they want to. I want them to be able to major in something that will pay them peanuts if it makes them happy. I want them to have a totally over-the-top wedding if that's what makes them happy." Almost looking vulnerable, he looked at me. I wasn't used to seeing vulnerability on him—it was a look I doubted more than a few people were used to seeing on him. "I just want to take care of them the way our parents would have."

My eyes were stinging from fighting tears. When I'd gotten up this morning and agreed to breakfast with Luke Archer, I hadn't known he was going to open up like this.

Luke Archer was so much more than a player setting batting records. So much more than a skilled lover. So much more.

"You really are amazing," I said.

Archer twisted his hat back around and leaned across the table a little. His expression was playful. "Well, I know that, but would you mind passing that on to this girl I'm really into? I'm not sure she's aware of that yet. She kind of busts my balls. When she's not icing them."

That made me laugh. "I think she knows."

"Good, and while you've got her on the line, would you mind asking her how I'm doing on our first date? I just spent the majority of it on the phone with a heartbroken sister and bringing up my dark past. I think I'm bombing it."

Archer's hand was resting on the table and I didn't realize I'd reached for it until our fingers were tying together. "She says it's the best first date she's ever been on."

chapter Twelve

THE SHOCK WAS back in San Diego, and everyone was excited to be playing in front of a home group of fans. We'd all gotten in late last night, and Archer had headed back to his apartment to meet his sisters, who had gotten into the city earlier and were waiting for him, while I went home to my empty apartment. Homecomings like this reminded me why I loved being on the road so much—it made me forget about just how alone I was.

It wasn't possible for me to go to his place with his sisters there. It wouldn't have been possible even if they weren't. While he was in Shock territory, cameras followed him everywhere short of the public restroom, and it wouldn't take long for people to figure out that the petite blonde he was with was the same one in her first year as an athletic trainer on the team he played for. We'd be safer in other cities, not that safe was any way of putting it.

After spending a fitful night as a human cyclone in my bed, I decided to head to Shock Stadium a couple hours early for lack of anything else to occupy my time.

Opening the door to my apartment, I found a box on the stoop, wrapped in the Shock's royal blue and white, along with a card with my name on it tucked under the bow. Kneeling, I opened the card:

Couldn't sleep last night. Maybe I'll sleep better tonight knowing you're in this.

It was signed 'Archer' in big bold letters, which seemed like a strange way to sign a person's name. Checking around to make sure I wasn't about to lift a racy scrap of lingerie out of the box in front of any neighbors, I pulled the ribbon free and opened the box.

The same big, bold letters stared at me from within the box, right above the number eleven, stitched on a Shock jersey. Lingerie—Luke Archer style.

Pulling it out, I let the jersey unfold in front of me. I wanted to put it on now. I wanted to wear it for the game today, like thousands of other fans who would be wearing Archer's number eleven on their backs.

I wanted what I couldn't have.

Letting out a sigh, I folded the jersey back up and set the box inside my apartment before I locked the door and headed to the stadium. For now, I'd have to leave Luke Archer to the fans.

I was the first one in the locker room, not that that was a first. I knew who would be the second to arrive. Luke always showed up way before the rest of the players. He had his ritual and routine before a game, although today's routine would include another ice bath.

The moment his eyes landed on me when I emerged from the room we kept the ice tubs in, his face fell.

"Nice to see you too," I greeted, trying to ignore the way my stomach was knotting from seeing him.

"You're not wearing my jersey."

"Did you actually think I would? Or that I could?"

"I guess not." His shoulders sagged. He was pouting. Luke Archer pouted.

"If it makes you feel any better, I'll be sure to wear it to bed tonight."

His eyes darkened. "You know what would make me feel even better?" He didn't wait for me to respond. "If it's *all* you wore to bed tonight."

I had to remind myself where I was and who would be arriving soon—the entire Shock brigade of players and staff.

"Deal," I said, waving into the room where the bath was ready for him. "The bath's ready whenever you are. Fifteen minutes in there, then we'll hit you with a heat treatment."

When he dropped his sports bag at the foot of his locker, hanging his cap up before tugging off his tee, I backed up a few steps.

Space seemed like a good thing right then.

"How's your leg doing?" I asked, diverting my gaze when his fingers dropped to his jeans.

"Fantastic, thanks to your tender loving care." His words were dripping insinuation.

"No pain?" I lifted a brow, doubtful. The kind of pull

he'd sustained didn't just go away as suddenly as it had happened.

"None."

"Comfortable putting your weight on it?"

"I'm comfortable putting my weight on it, supporting someone else's weight on it . . ." He made sure I was looking before he dropped his jeans. And shit. He was commando. And at full staff. More space between us seemed like an even better idea.

"How are your sisters?" I gave an innocent smile and waited.

His face fell. Other parts of his anatomy, not so much. "You're cruel."

"And you've got a date with a tub full of ice. Let me know when you're out." Snagging the clipboard from outside Coach's office, I pretended to be focused on the lineup for the day as I headed into the supply room.

"Hey, Doc?"

I paused.

"Are you going to clear me to play today?"

My teeth worked that out on my lip for a moment before I turned to face him. This was what I'd been worried about with us. Or one of the things I'd been worried about. That I'd let my feelings for him get in the way of doing my job. As Allie, the woman in a relationship with him, I knew he wanted to play and had the grit and stamina to do so. It was a home game after a long stretch on the road, and his sisters would be in the stands, hoping to cheer on their big brother. Allie wanted him to play. Allie knew he could play.

The athletic trainer knew playing today was pushing it. The kind of pull he'd sustained generally required more rest, and the risk of him reinjuring it and putting him in even worse shape was a very real possibility. The athletic trainer felt conflicted. Part of her felt like sitting out another game would mitigate the risk, and another part knew Luke Archer was capable of more than just any other player.

I was in a difficult position, knowing I'd upset him and the rest of the team if I advised him to sit this one out too. I was in a difficult situation if I gave him the green light to play and he really messed up his leg.

"Before you say anything, I just want you to know that I've been thinking about what you said to me a few days ago in the shower room."

"We didn't say much from what I remember." I clutched the clipboard to my chest, trying to ignore the fact that the man who knew how to do wonderful things to my body with his body was naked and ready fifteen feet in front of me.

"No, but what you did say left an impression."

"Good to know you were listening."

Archer folded his jeans and stuffed them inside his locker. "I want you to know that I respect that you have a job to do and that you can't let us get in the way of that." He waved his finger between us. "It's your call, Doc. I'm not going to pressure you either way, and I'm not going to sulk if you tell the coach to bench me." He let those words hang between us for a moment before grabbing a towel and heading back toward the tubs. "I've said what I needed to. I'll be turning my *huevos* into ice cubes if you need me."

"Big baby," I muttered after him.

His chuckle echoed from the back room.

After that, players and staff slowly filtered into the locker room, the buzz zapping in the air from the thrill of a home game. Archer took care of timing himself in the bath and the heat compress that followed, leaving me time to tend to some of the other players.

"Eden!" Coach Beckett's deep voice boomed through the locker room.

"Yeah, Coach?" I replied as I finished taping Robinson's shoulder.

"In my office," he shouted before storming back in there.

Coach's temperament had taken me a while to get used to, but now I barely flinched when he hollered at me. That was just the way he worked. I didn't doubt he hollered good night to his wife every night before crawling under the covers.

Stretching the last piece of tape over Robert's shoulder, I jogged into Coach's office, guessing I already knew what he wanted to talk to me about.

"Close the door," he said, spreading his hands on his desk as I entered.

After closing the door, I moved in front of his desk and remained standing. Usually my meetings with Coach were too short to sit.

"Archer. Is he playing tonight or not?"

My mind raced, as conflicted now as it had been earlier. I knew he'd be asking and I knew I'd be expected to give him an answer. I just wasn't sure what that answer was yet.

"No bullshit either, Eden. If Archer can play, he plays. If he can't, his ass will stay on that bench. I want it straight." Coach's cleats echoed through the office when he shifted his weight.

My mind undulated from one answer to the other. Could Archer play? Yes, he could. *Should* Archer play? That was a trickier answer.

"He can play." My voice sounded smaller than I wanted to, so I gave it another try. "He can play."

Coach was quiet for a minute, his eyes challenging me, giving me a chance to retract my statement. When I didn't, his finger lifted at me. "If my star player reinjures himself and puts him out for the season, it's going to be your ass on the line, Eden. You understand?"

I swallowed, nodding. "I understand."

chapter *Thirteen*

THE SHOCK HAD dominated all night long. Fielding, batting, running, scoring—they'd owned the game against the Seattle Sharks, proving why they were the favorite to win the Series this year.

After the loss to New Orleans, the team needed this win. The energy in the dugout had been overwhelming, largely due to one number eleven being elated he was back to playing the sport he loved.

When Coach had told Archer he was on for tonight, he'd run a circle around the locker room, high-fiving every member of the team and staff. He saved me for last, managing to give my hand a little squeeze in passing.

We were at the top of the ninth with only one out left to pretty much win the game since we were up eight runs, and I was thinking about finally relaxing. The whole night I'd been watching Archer's every move, looking for any signs of him favoring his right leg, but all of the worry and vigilance had been for nothing.

Archer was moving just fine, clipping around the bases at his usual speed, fielding balls with no signs of pain or injury. I'd made the right call. He'd told me he was ready, I'd assessed he was, and I'd made a good call.

I knew not every aspect of my job had guarantees and certainties, but I couldn't take the pressure off of myself.

The Sharks' batter had just earned his second strike, and the guys in the dugout were holding their breaths, ready to celebrate. The next pitch Watson threw, the batter connected with, sending a whizzing line drive right between first and second.

From the dugout, it looked like the right fielder would have to field it, but Archer blurred into motion, making a sharp turn to get to it before leaping into the air. The ball whacked into his mitt right before he went crashing to the ground, a billow of dust erupting around him.

The game was over—the Shock had won.

I wasn't sure who went wilder: the crowd or the team. The players left in the dugout rushed the field while the crestfallen Sharks trudged off of it. The coaching staff was clapping each other's backs while the medical staff was giving our usual sighs of relief that the game was over and every player who'd walked onto the field was able to walk off of it.

That was when my gaze drifted toward first base, where Archer was being righted by a herd of his fellow players, shouting their *Hell yeah's* and clapping him on the shoulder. No one else seemed to notice, but I did. The subtle flash of pain pull at his face when he started walking off the field with his teammates. The set of his jaw when he put weight on his right leg with each step.

Shit. Slinging my bag over my body, I rushed out of the dugout and onto the field. The players passed me with celebration on their faces, nudging my shoulders as I passed them. No one seemed to notice that one of their players was in pain.

When Archer saw me loping toward him, his eyes darted toward the dugout, where Coach was. I didn't miss the relief that washed over his face with whatever he saw.

Squeezing between him and Watson, my eyes locked on his.

"I'm fine," he said under his breath.

"Liar," I whispered back, moving to put my shoulder under his arm to help him off the field.

"No, don't." He gave an almost indiscreet shake of his head. "Coach—I don't want him to know."

"Afraid he's going to yell at you?" The noise was so loud in the stadium, I had to put my mouth right outside his ear for him to hear me.

Archer's jaw set a little more. "I don't care if he yells at me—I'm used to it. I don't like the idea of him yelling at you though."

I huffed, matching his every step off the field with one of my own. "I can take it."

"I can't."

If he thought Coach would have something to yell at me over, that meant he'd hurt his leg. Again. For all I knew, he'd pulled it all over again.

"Don't," he said under his breath when I moved to support some of his weight again.

"Dammit, Luke, this is my job."

"Exactly, and I want to make sure you still have one tomorrow." He tipped his chin just enough as we moved toward Coach. He was watching us now.

"How bad is it?"

"Not bad." When I started to exhale, he added, "Really."

"Is that why I can see beads of sweat forming on your forehead?"

The faintest of smiles crept into place. "I just finished playing nine innings. Sweat usually comes with the game."

"Are those nine innings the same reason you look ready to crack a few molars from the way you're grinding your jaw?"

Coach was still watching us, his brow furrowed just enough to give away that he suspected something was up. Picking up on the same, Luke's strides became stronger, his gait less uneven.

"How bad? Really?" I asked.

"Not bad. Just a little mad."

I guessed he was lying or at least under-exaggerating. I guessed that had he been anyone else, he would have been curled up in a ball on the ground, crying for a painkiller that would knock out a Thoroughbred.

That was when his gaze wandered to the stands, centering on one of the front rows, where three girls were flailing their arms like they were trying to hail a cab in New York during rush hour. If he hadn't told me he had three little sisters, I would have figured it out from one look at them. They were all mini girl versions of Luke:

light brown hair, big expressive eyes, and the same wide smiles.

"Fan club?" I asked when he returned the arm flailing motion.

"The feeling's mutual."

His sisters were winding their way to the fence, waving him over, totally decked out with Shock gear from foam fingers to shoelaces.

"Why don't you go say hi, and I'll get your ice bath ready?"

Luke groaned, but it wasn't very convincing with the smile on his face. "You want to come meet them?"

My feet stopped moving. He paused when he noticed me stopped at the edge of the field. Since I still didn't know how to define whatever we were, family introductions had been way off my radar. Introducing a person to one's family meant things were serious enough to bring that person into your inner circle. Was that how Luke felt about us? Or was he just being polite?

How did *I* feel about us?

"I think they want to see their brother right now," I said. "Not one of the team's athletic trainers."

Luke's shoulder lifted. "They'd definitely be interested in meeting the woman I'm seeing."

"Are you sure you're ready for this?'

His eyes locked on mine. "Sometimes the only way to know if you're ready is to take the leap."

chapter Fourteen

"I'M SORRY I put you on the spot like that," Luke said from the second-row seat of his SUV while I sat in the driver's seat, feeling like I was driving a tank down the interstate.

"You didn't put me on the spot. There was just a lot coming at me at that particular moment in time."

"Like me suggesting I introduce you to my sisters."

I sagged in relief when he pointed at the upcoming exit sign. In addition to feeling like a bus in comparison to my small sedan, Luke's SUV wasn't a smooth ride. My body would probably still be vibrating tomorrow morning. "Like me realizing I made a bad call letting you play tonight."

"You didn't make a bad call."

As he said it, I heard him adjust the bag of ice I'd forced him to keep on his leg. I'd also insisted he keep it elevated for the next twenty-four hours, which was why I was in my current condition—barreling a tank off the interstate while Luke Archer sat behind me with a reinjured groin muscle.

"Is that why you didn't want to say anything to Coach about it?" I asked.

Our eyes connected in the rear view mirror.

"I didn't want to say anything to him because there was nothing to report."

"And that's the reason you have a bag of ice on your crotch and are laid out in the backseat, right?"

He leaned forward, bracing his hands between the passenger and driver's seats. He smelled fresh from the shower, his still-wet hair curling around the rim of his ball cap.

Getting distracted by the way Luke smelled was not a great idea if I placed a priority on getting him to a destination safe and in one piece.

"No, *you* are the reason I have a bag of frozen water on my crotch." His fingers curled into my headrest caressed my cheek. "I'd much rather have something else between them right now."

"Like a vise?"

Archer chuckled, pointing me down the right road when we came to the end of the off-ramp. "Hey, Allie?"

"Mm-hmm?"

"Thank you."

"For what?"

"For letting me play. For taking a chance on me. For being you." His hand dropped to my shoulder and gave it a squeeze.

"Is that all?"

"No, not all, but it sums up a good chunk of my thanks." He pointed down the next road, and I coaxed the tank into a turn.

"In that case, you're welcome." I tried not to get distracted by him in the rearview mirror. Or the way I could feel him leaning toward me. Or the way his hand was still lingering on my shoulder. "Can I ask you a weird question?"

"I'd be disappointed if you asked me one that wasn't weird."

I lifted my brow at him in the rearview mirror. "The condom thing." I swallowed. "Pulling out last time . . . what's the deal? I've never met a guy so concerned with birth control."

Luke didn't look the slightest bit uncomfortable with the topic when I checked the mirror.

"Do you not trust me—what I said about being covered? Do you just really like latex? Are you scared of having a kid?" My eyes stayed on the road after that. I felt all kinds of awkward bringing this up, but it had been on my mind ever since that first night. I appreciated him being so responsible, but there was a difference between conscientious and paranoid.

"No, none of that. I trust you—I wouldn't be with you like that if I didn't. I don't have some latex fetish, and I'm not scared of having a kid." Luke was quiet for a minute, so I checked the mirror—he was staring out the side window with a pensive expression. "I'm scared of getting a woman pregnant who isn't sure she wants me in her life."

My eyebrows came together. "But that isn't me. That

wouldn't be me if that happened."

Luke pointed at a tall building up ahead, so I moved into the right lane. "But until I knew that, I had to be careful. You may think you know a person, but you need to *know* you know a person."

When I looked at him in the mirror, this time he glanced away. Whatever was playing out in his eyes, he didn't want me to see.

"Why?" I asked.

His jaw set as I pulled up in front of his apartment building.

"Another time," he said at last, shifting in the backseat. "I'd invite you up but . . ."

"You have three younger sisters at your place?" Putting the tank in park, I twisted around in my seat. His expression was clearing from the topic we'd just touched on, but it was obvious there was a story there. Maybe one day he'd feel comfortable enough to tell me. Maybe he never would. After the way Ben treated me, I knew what it felt like to have scars you wanted to keep hidden.

"Actually . . . I figured you'd say no," he said, gesturing toward the front doors to his building.

"Oh."

"Am I wrong?" Bracing his elbows against the headrests of the front seats, he leaned forward.

"No, you're right," I said, trying to ignore that his face wasn't even a foot away from mine. "I'm sure your sisters want you all to themselves right now."

He gave me a minute to change my mind—clearly trying to change it for me with the way he was looking at me—then shrugged. "Okay. Thanks for the ride."

As he crawled across the backseat to open the door, something hit me. "I just realized something," I said, blinking. "I have no idea how I'm going to get back to my car to get home."

Archer's smile told me this had crossed his mind a while ago. "Just realized that, eh? I was wondering how long it would take you to figure it out. Must have been distracted by something." Waggling his brows, he added, "Or someone."

"The man stretched out on the backseat should not be flattering himself right now."

He chuckled like my state of transportation impairment was amusement at its best. "Take my car home," he said, motioning at the steering wheel. "We can go get your car together tomorrow."

"I don't want to drive this tank another length of curb."

His mouth fell open. "Are you insulting my wheels?"

"Yeah, I think I am." Even in park, the thing was rumbling like we were four-wheeling up some logging road. "Besides, why are you driving something that probably rolled off the manufacturing line when we were in middle school?"

"Because we have a lot of history." He patted the passenger seat affectionately. "I drove this baby to college my freshman year. It's gotten me through a lot of good times. You don't just abandon it because people expect you to drive a Range Rover with twenty-inch rims." He made a face like he'd rather be caught driving a hot pink Barbie car. "Besides, in this, I'm incognito. As you've just proven, no one expects me to be driving a 2003 Tahoe."

Maybe I shouldn't have been surprised a guy who made bank drove a car with a trade-in value of probably five grand, but it still made me shake my head. "Point made."

"So I'll see you tomorrow morning then? Around eight?" His hand dropped on the back door handle.

"To drop off your car?"

His shoulders lifted. "And to go shopping. Remember? Me and the girls. At the mall all day."

I exhaled. "I don't know, Luke."

"Come on, it'll be fun. Plus, if you expect me to follow-through on my promise to keep my leg elevated all day, that means I'll be in a wheelchair, which means shopping will be spatially challenging."

I made a face at him. "Spatially challenging?"

"Have you ever been in those teen girl stores?" He waited like he was expecting an answer. I didn't think my abundance of team polos and khakis required an answer to that. "I can barely fit as a bi-ped. Definitely won't be able to as a four-wheeler with an appendage hanging out."

"Speaking of appendages . . ."

His smile twisted as his eyes dropped to his crotch. "I thought you'd never ask."

"How is your leg?" I said around a sigh. Luke had a one-track mind that was always heading in the same direction—between my legs.

"Better than my dick right now," he muttered, looking so dejected I had to bite my cheek to keep from laughing.

As he started shoving the door open, sliding down the seat to leave, I made a spur-of-the-moment decision. One I hoped I wouldn't regret.

"Luke?" When he glanced back over his shoulder, I said, "I'll see you tomorrow."

All signs of dejection disappeared instantly. "Really?"

Instead of overthinking it, I listened to what my heart was telling me. "Really."

chapter Fifteen

FROM THE SOUNDS I could hear coming from the other side of the door, it sounded like an entire mob of sorority sisters had taken over Luke's apartment. Some over-played, under-talented band's song was blaring, a couple of girls' voices joining in during the chorus. The sound of a blow dryer could be made out in the background, and I just heard someone close to panic levels shrieking about their missing tube of mascara.

It even smelled like a sorority house—or walking past the threshold of a Bath and Body Works and getting plowed over by the array of scents blasting out.

Thinking of Luke inside with three teenage girls who sounded and smelled as though they were fully embracing their teenage state of being made me smile. He came across as such a guy's guy on and off the field, so hanging with him and his sisters today should be an enlightening experience.

That was part of the reason I'd agreed to it—I wanted

to see him in a different element. I wanted to see how he was and who he was with his family. Was the man I knew the same one he was with those he loved the most? If not, who was the real Luke Archer—the one I knew or the one I was about to get a glimpse of?

The other reason I'd agreed was because I knew I would miss him. It was too early on in a relationship to be missing someone, but that didn't change the fact that I wanted to be around him on our days off. It wasn't just the intimacy I wanted—it was his presence. The energy he exuded, his easy smiles, and the way one look from him could make me feel things in every part of my body.

Managing to maneuver the tank into a parking space in the garage this morning after slogging it back to my place last night, I made my way up to his apartment. A doorman buzzing residents or visitors in was about as fancy as the building got. Never would anyone look at it and think one of the top players in the game of baseball lived here. I loved that he did though. I loved that he drove a decade-old vehicle and lived in the kind of place that appealed to the middle-class of the city. I loved that for Luke, playing was about the sport—not the money and fame that came with it.

When the song changed to one that made me cringe, I heard Luke's moan of protest from the other side of the door. Good to know neither of us would force the other to listen to this atrocity.

I'd stalled long enough, so I knocked on the door. Luke had mentioned leaving around nine, and it was only a few minutes to. Plus, I had to get him situated in his mode of transportation for the day.

When the door flew open, the first thing the girl's eyes drifted to was the wheelchair in front of me. Then she busted up.

"Please say that's for Luke," she greeted, stepping aside and waving me in.

"It's for Luke."

"And all is right in the universe again." She was the female version of Luke—striking eyes, long caramel-colored hair, and an easy smile. She had a small gold necklace on with her name hanging from it. For a girl who'd just had her heart broken, she looked like it was already healed. To be young again.

"Where is the gimp?"

"Probably hiding in his closet with a pillow wrapped around his head." She closed the door behind me and padded into the living room.

It looked like a sorority house too. Nail polish bottles were scattered over the end tables, pillows were strewn around like a pillow fight had just gone down, and articles of clothing were hanging and scattered across every stationary surface, including the television.

"Cameron!" she shouted down a hall. "Turn it down! Luke's trainer is here!" She waited until the volume dialed down. "Sorry, I'm Alex, and you must be Allie." Her eyes dropped to the wheelchair.

Luke and I had agreed via a quick text this morning to keep our relationship quiet with the girls. To them, I was an athletic trainer for his team and nothing more. That was it. Not because I was worried about them blasting it out there for everyone to know, but because bringing a person into their family circle was a big deal. I didn't want Luke to introduce me to his sisters as the woman he was seeing until I'd caught up to what was going on between us. Until I could qualify what it was and determine if there was a few-weeks expiration date.

"Nice to meet you, Alex. All set for shopping?"

She lifted a foot, which she already had her sneaker tied onto. "I've got my shopping shoes on and everything. Maximum speed. Minimum fatigue."

I was reconsidering my own shoe choice—I saw just how serious this girl was about her shopping—when I felt it. His presence. His stare. His nearness. I wasn't sure what exactly it was that I felt, but I knew he was close and he was watching me.

I tried to paint the most unaffected of looks on my face before glancing up. That plan lasted a whole half second before my eyes connected with his.

He was standing in the middle of the hall, watching me like no one was around . . . like three of his sisters. When his eyes dropped from mine to examine what I was wearing, his arm jetted out, his hand molding against the wall like he was bracing himself.

His eyes had some sort of direct connection to every nerve ending in my possession. They all fired to life at the same time, making it both impossible to stay frozen in place and to move.

"Hey." He gave me a smile that wasn't exactly "little sister appropriate" as he started down the hall toward me.

But when I detected his subtle limp, the trainer in me

resurfaced. "What are you doing on your feet?"

Behind me, Alex popped off a, "Busted."

"Walking," Luke answered with an easy shrug. "I've been doing it for twenty-four years now. Mastered it twenty-three years ago. Been doing it ever since."

"And if you want to keep walking, I'd suggest you get in this thing and keep your leg elevated for the rest of the day like you promised me." Rolling the wheelchair toward him, I tried out a glare on him. It was a weak attempt, made weaker still when his eyes continued to roam me. When they reached the hem of my summer dress, the crease in his forehead told me exactly what he was imagining.

"Did you two already meet?" Luke cleared his throat.

"Yep, and she's my new favorite person since she's going to make you ride in this all day. Your throne awaits, Grandpa."

Luke threw Alex an annoyed look, but it was the kind that was borne from affection. "Yeah, yeah. I'd watch it with the teasing since Grandpa here is the one with the credit cards in his wallet."

With that, Alex sealed her lips and painted on a sweet smile.

"Cameron! Gaby! I want you to meet someone!" he called.

Luke's jaw set when his gaze dropped to the neckline of my dress. There wasn't anything special about the dress I'd slipped into this morning. No plunging necklines. No hems that floated closer to the ass than the knee. No clingy places that threatened to cut off circulation to my upper or lower half. Feminine maybe, but the dress was definitely not sexy. But I supposed compared to the khakis and polo shirts Luke typically saw me in, this was the red light attire equivalent.

From the last look he'd given me before turning around and planting his butt in the wheelchair, I was confident he had plans that included ripping my dress off instead of removing it . . . after a full day of shopping and getting his sisters to the airport later tonight.

After coming around the front of the chair, I lowered to get the leg rest adjusted to fit him. His mouth curled up on one side as he took in the view of me on my knees in front of him.

"Don't make me ice you," I whispered, my eyes dropping to his crotch, when Alex wandered into the kitchen.

"Don't make me have to do even filthier things to you in my head than I'm already doing." His brow lifted at me, my hand still wrapped around his ankle even after getting his leg settled into place. "Although I think the red impression of my hand on your ass would be something to behold. I think I'd need to take a picture of it so I can blow it up, hang it on the ceiling above my bed, and fall asleep each night to the sight of my hand print on your perfect ass."

My throat went dry, my heartbeat vibrating in my ears. Scanning the area, I found it sister-free, but it wouldn't stay that way for long. Saying the kinds of things he was, giving me the kinds of looks he was, when we had a good fifteen hours before we could be together was cruel.

When he observed how I was responding to his words, a smirk worked into place. Fine. He wanted to start the foreplay this early in the day, I'd return the favor. Checking the room to make sure his sisters were still missing, I crawled forward on my knees until I was more between his legs than in front of them. I gave a little tug on my dress, and Luke's eyes darted to the freshly exposed shadow of my cleavage.

"If you think what you're imaging right now is filthy," I whispered, my eyes lowering to the spot between his legs. I moved closer, right into the same position I'd be in if I was about to go down on him. "You should hear what I imagined last night." When my gaze lifted from the growing mass between his legs, I found his breathing speeding up, his pupils dilated, his expression similar to the one I saw whenever he thrust inside me for the first time. "While I was touching myself. Wearing your jersey."

My eyes held his for another moment before I popped to a stand, gave his leg a pat, and pretended like nothing had happened between us. Just in time. A door at the end of the hall exploded open, and a couple of girls spilled out, the music having come to a merciful end.

Blinking a few times, Luke caught up to my nothing-just-happened façade. "Cameron, Gaby, this is Allie." He waved between us, but his voice was higher than normal. I gloated on the inside from knowing I'd riled him up. "Allie, these are my sisters."

At the same time, the girls seemed to notice Luke was in a wheelchair. Like Alex, they both started laughing, exchanging a high five, to which Luke responded with a light-hearted grumble.

"Not cool to laugh at people in wheelchairs," he said with a wounded look.

"We're not laughing at people in wheelchairs. We're laughing at *you* in a wheelchair," Cameron, who appeared to be the middle sister, piped up. "I've never even seen you put a Band-Aid on, and you're actually going to spend a whole day in this because you have an itty-bitty baby muscle in your leg that hurts?"

Luke gave a sigh. "I'm doing what my athletic trainer advised me to do."

"Since when?"

Luke feigned being appalled. "Since always."

That was when Alex came back into the room, clutching a bottle of water. "Since never."

"You didn't tell us she was a girl," Cameron said.

Cameron and Gaby rolled to a stop in front of Luke, crossing their arms and giving him a look that was all accusation.

"I didn't realize I had to."

"You didn't tell us she was a *pretty* girl," Gaby said in a tone that made it seem like we were in some sort of interrogation room.

If his three sisters teaming up against him was getting to him, it didn't show. He didn't shift and the corners of his eyes didn't crease—almost like he had plenty of experience keeping secret lovers veiled from his family.

"She's the best athletic trainer on the team. I'd list a dozen qualities about her before her aesthetics, as nice as they are." When he glanced at me, his gaze stayed there for a couple moments too long.

"You didn't tell us you couldn't not look at her and get a stupid smile on your face." Alex shouldered up beside her sisters, circling her finger at Luke who, yeah, kind of had a stupid smile.

I looked away so I could bite my smile into submission before my act was blown by three of the most perceptive teens I'd ever met.

"Are you ready to go shopping or what? Because you shouldn't *keep* teasing the person with the credit cards in his back pocket."

"Threats." Alex tipped her head. "So very idle coming from you."

Luke groaned, shrugging deeper into the wheelchair. "We haven't even gotten to the mall and I'm already in agony."

"Then what are we waiting for?" Gaby clapped excitedly, almost sprinting for the door.

"Archer sisters?" I almost had to shout over the shrieks of excitement as purses were thrown around shoulders and sandals slid into. "Ever wanted to play dress-up with your big brother?" Tugging on the bag I'd slung around the back of the wheelchair, I unzipped it.

"Ever? I'll be in therapy until I'm eighty from the years of psychological damage they did in the name of dress-up."

Seeing I had the girls' attention, I ignored Luke's complaints and dumped the contents of the bag on the floor. "Since I doubt I can push this load faster than the paparazzi can chase us, and I'm guessing you want to shop all day long"—I continued through another one of his grumbles—"we need a disguise."

When the sisters saw what I'd brought along to disguise their brother with, they bounced in place. When Luke twisted his head over his shoulder to see what I had planned, he frowned.

"Oh, hell no."

chapter Sixteen

"GO, SHOCK!" A crowd of guys shouted as they passed us later that morning at the mall. Or they shouted as they passed a certain sullen-faced someone in a wheelchair.

"Go back to Orlando," another grunted at us. Or at Luke.

I'd lost track of all the irritated groans from passers-by, but they'd kept pace with the delighted giggles from the three Archer sisters.

"Why don't you fly a Rays flag off of this thing so we can draw a little more attention?" Luke waved at the elderly woman we passed next, who was shaking her head at him like he'd just spilled grape juice on her floral settee.

"You know, I think there's a sport's memorabilia store not too far up ahead. We could use a flag, don't you think, ladies?"

Three heads bobbed in eager agreement.

"That was a sarcastic suggestion. You know, since

your sense of humor is clearly off-kilter." Archer tipped his ball cap at the next bunch of guys who were wearing ball caps of their own. Of the rival team—the San Diego Shock. "I thought the point was not to draw attention to me."

"Go Shock!" I hollered with the passing bunch, flicking the bill of the black-and-orange cap Luke had on. "Nope. The point was to not draw attention to Luke Archer, batting legend for the San Diego Shock."

"Exactly. You can draw as much attention as you want for being the chump diehard fan of the rival team in the Shock's home city." Alex, who was taking a turn wheeling Luke through the mall, winked at me.

"Clearly," Luke said, pinching the Orlando Rays jersey we'd forced him into as if its mere existence offended him.

We hadn't stopped at the jersey though. We'd dropped a Ray's ball cap on his head, hung a foam finger off of one of the wheelchair arms, and tied about a mile's worth of black and orange streamers all up and around the wheelchair. Luke Archer was officially the Orlando Rays biggest fan, and it was about to cause a mutiny in San Diego, where fans bled Shock royal blue.

"Ooh, we're here!" Cameron skidded to a stop in front of a store that I'd guess was meant for teens, but judging from the clothes on the mannequins in the front windows, it looked more like toddler-sized clothing. Like the handful of other shops we'd already been in, it was packed to overflowing with racks and rounders of cut-offs and tanks.

Luke and I winced together while the three girls sprinted inside.

"Have fun," he said, holding out his shiny black card in my direction.

"How many pairs of denim shorts can a girl own?"

"Apparently there isn't a limit." Luke gave a thumbs-up when Gaby waved yet another pair of cut-offs at him through the store's window. As I started weaving into the store of toddler-sized clothes meant to be worn by teenagers, he called, "Hey, Allie?"

"Hey, yeah?" I spun around.

"Thank you for doing this. Well, not for doing *this*"—he waved at himself in all his black-and-orange glory—"but for coming with us today. It might not seem like a big deal, but it is. To me. So thank you."

My feet carried me back to him before I knew I was going. My fingers tangled through his before I knew they'd reached for him. "It's nice to see this side of you. The non-baseball-legend side." My spine shot with sensation when his thumb caressed the inside of my wrist.

"It's nice to have you see this side of me."

"You're a pretty amazing brother. I hope you know that."

Luke's eyes diverted into the store, where I guessed another sister was flashing him something else. His answer to every piece of clothing had been a thumbs-up. Never a thumbs-down. Every girl needed a guy in her life who always gave her the thumbs-up, no matter what. Luke's sisters were lucky.

"They're amazing. They just make me look good."

"Says the brother who would pay any price, financially or personally, for any one of them." Giving his hand a squeeze, I turned back toward the store. "Have fun getting booed at here. Those Shock and Archer fans are brutal."

He gave me a disparaging look right before something wicked flashed in his eyes. "After this, I'm going to feel a lot less guilty about leaving that red handprint on your ass tonight."

"Mall. People." I flourished my hands up and down at the hall we were in, droves of shoppers passing by.

Luke lifted a brow. "So?

"Never mind." I sighed before going in search of three teenage girls.

If experience had anything to do with it, they were probably already throwing on clothes in the dressing room. None of them even eighteen and they'd already mastered the art of power shopping.

Wandering through the store, I found Alex perusing a rounder of vintage-style tees—the other two must have beaten her to the dressing room.

"I'm armed and loaded with a limitless credit card, so go crazy." I came up on the other side of the rounder. "How's it going?"

"Eggplant or charcoal?" She held up two tees, taking a turn floating each one over her so I could get the full effect.

"Both," I suggested.

"Nah." She shook her head, studying the shirts before putting the charcoal one back. "Luke already does way too much for us."

Glancing at the tag of one of the shirts, I saw the price was less than ten bucks each. As fiends of shopping and fashion as the girls clearly were, none of them had gone crazy setting registers on fire. At all. A few pairs of cut-offs and a few shirts each, but all of them seemed to behave like they had a budget.

"I don't think twenty bucks for a couple of shirts is going to raise your brother's brow. Not even a little bit."

"I know. But . . ."

"Do you know how much—"

"Twenty-one million dollars a year?" Her eyes lifted from the rack of dresses she was thumbing through. "Yeah, I know how much he makes. It's not about the money. It's about everything he's done for all of us ever since—" She stopped herself short, chewing it out on her lip for a moment. "Do you know about what happened?"

"To your parents?" I asked softly, and she nodded. "Yes, he told me."

"After that, the three of us could have gone and lived with other family. But we would have had to move away from home, from our friends, our schools. The places we used to go to with Dad and Mom." She pulled out a dress, but she was obviously seeing something else when she studied the chevron print. "Luke kept us all together. In the same home we grew up in. He talked with Anne and brought her in to take care of us since he couldn't be home with us for most of the year. He made it so that even though we'd lost our parents, we didn't have to lose everything else too. It's not about the money. I already owe Luke more than I could ever hope to pay back." This time when she worked at her bottom lip, I guessed it was to ward off tears. "Does that make any sense at all?"

"Hey, as someone who can't take a compliment without feeling like I owe a person big time, I so get it." I paused to collect my thoughts. "But love isn't about owing a person or feeling in their debt. It's about giving what you can, when you can, and allowing that in return. It's not all a matter of the head—it's just as much a matter of the heart."

Alex shifted, hanging the dress back up. "So are you saying to buy both of the shirts?"

I smiled. "Not exactly. What I'm trying to say is just accept what he can and wants to give you without worrying about how you'll pay him back. Just like you'd want him to accept what you can and want to give him without worrying about how he'll pay you back." I felt my forehead crease as I replayed what I'd said to a seventeen-year-old I'd just met smack in the middle of a store that was blasting yet more reprehensible music. "Does that make sense? Because now that I'm rethinking it, I don't know what I just said."

Alex laughed, moving on to the next rack. "You're saying that we all might express it uniquely, but it comes down to the same thing—love."

"Exactly what I'm saying."

"Glad we cleared that up."

A teenage girl who'd been on a handful of dates in her life apparently knew more about the inner workings of love than I did—a grown woman who'd known her fair share of relationships. That was a depressing thought. A sobering reality. I remembered thinking I knew what love was, but somewhere along the way, I'd lost it. Its definition had been skewed by Ben and my subsequent failed relationships. Somewhere along life's journey, I'd lost the essence of love. The simplicity of it had been lost, hidden by conditions, masked by doubt, veiled by qualifiers.

Here, in this toddler-clothing-sized store, with this young girl, I'd just remembered it. You either loved a person or you didn't. They either loved you or they didn't. Time didn't play a role in it, and neither did circumstance.

It wasn't a decision you came to logically; it was a feeling you knew instinctively.

The next realization that hit me had me reaching for a rack to keep myself from teetering in place. Thankfully, my stream of thoughts was interrupted.

"How is he?" Alex glanced out the front of the store where we could just make out Luke. Who was getting another round of jeers from fans in Shock caps. He responded with a peace sign.

"Good," I answered, moving with her to the next rounder of shirts. "He's having an amazing season. Setting some records already. Other than the muscle strain, he's been great."

"I watch every game. I know every stat. That's not what I'm asking about. How is *Luke*, my brother? Not Luke Archer, the baseball player."

"Oh." When I held up a shirt with a baseball on it, she held out her hand to take it. "Why are you asking me?"

"Because you're on the team with him. You two must spend a lot of time together." Her eyes met mine and stayed there a moment. "And I maybe haven't missed the way you two look at each other." She glanced out into the mall where Luke was stationed, his gaze intent on us. "And the way you act around each other."

Maybe I should have been panicking that Luke's sister had just called us out, but then again, maybe I shouldn't gave gotten involved with a player on the same team I worked for. My should-have radar was seriously misfiring lately. "You just met me. How do you know that's not how I look at and act around everyone?"

"I don't." Alex lifted her shoulders. "But I do know the way my brother looks at and acts around people, and this isn't how he acts around everyone else."

I felt a smile tugging at the corners of my mouth. "Really?"

"Really."

"That obvious?"

"If it makes you feel better, I am especially observant." She lifted her hand at her sisters when they popped out of their dressing rooms and waved her over. Then she faced me with an expectant expression.

"He's good," I answered. "This is my first season with the team, so we're really just getting to know one another, but he seems good. Happy."

"Yeah?"

"Yeah."

"Good. That's a relief. Luke's been through a lot. Our parents. His career." She paused, her eyes moving to her brother. "Other stuff." I was just about to ask her what other stuff she was talking about when she added, "He spends all of his worry on us, but then who worries about him?"

"You do?" It wasn't a guess—it was obvious.

"Don't tell him." She lifted her finger to her lips. "He likes to think the three of us have nothing more to worry about than what color we want to paint our toenails and turning our homework in on time."

"Not a word," I promised.

As she headed for the dressing rooms, she waited for me to come up beside her. "So you guys are seeing each other?"

I guessed my long inhale was all the answer she needed.

"Can I talk in hypothetical terms?" she asked.

"If I can answer hypothetically."

"Fair's fair." She nudged my arm. "If you were seeing him, I'd tell you you're dating the best guy in the whole world."

"Yeah? Why would you say that?" Not that I was arguing, but I was curious to know why a teenage girl thought her big brother was the best guy in the world. Most girls her age thought some magazine-cover dude with tattoos and supposed swagger was the height of the male species.

"Because it's the truth. Luke takes care of people. He's loyal. He does the right thing." She squinted like she was trying to focus on something. "Sometimes to a fault."

I nodded. "I'll take that under advisement. Hypothetically. Anything else?"

A sales associate was helping Alex into a dressing

room beside her sisters, but before she closed the curtain, Alex stuck her head out. Those same hazel eyes I'd seen on her brother locked on mine. "Yeah, if you hurt him, you'll have three sisters to answer to."

chapter Seventeen

WE WERE BOTH exhausted. Spending twelve hours at a mall with three girls had a way of doing that to two people as averse to malls as Luke and I were. So would trying to eat as much mall food as one's stomach could hold without erupting. If I never saw another salted pretzel, tub of cheese sauce, or ice cream cone again, I'd be good.

We had just dropped the girls off at the airport after packing and picking up their luggage at Luke's apartment and were heading back to his place, both of us looking like we were in a state of mall shock and sleep deprivation. But as soon as we came within a block of his apartment building, our energy zapped to life.

He was still in the Ray's get-up, although he'd tossed the hat in the garbage can back at the airport, claiming he didn't give a shit if anyone recognized him without it. He just couldn't take another second of it on his head.

I'd never been so keenly aware of a man and his desire for me pulsing in waves over me. I'd never been so keenly aware of my own desire for a man, to the point of feeling like I was swallowing my heart with every breath.

Instead of pulling up to the front of the building as I had last night when dropping him off, I pulled into the garage. I told myself it was because wheeling him back to his apartment would take time, but I knew it was because I wasn't in a hurry to leave. Especially now that we were alone.

Turning off the ignition after pulling into his reserved parking space, I sat there, staring out the windshield, wondering if he could hear my heartbeat.

From the smirk I could see out of the corner of my eye, I guessed he could.

"So I kept my promise for the day, and if my ass never has to sit in one of those things again, it will be too damn soon."

I nodded. He had been a good sport about it, leaving me surprised all day. From the quid pro quo insinuation in his tone, I guessed I knew why he'd been so accommodating.

"So?" I shrugged like I didn't know what he was alluding to.

"So it's time for you to uphold your promise."

Damn. Just his voice was making me wetter. Or maybe it was the image of what his voice was hinting at.

"I didn't make you a promise."

"Just because you didn't verbalize it doesn't mean you didn't make one."

My hands wrung the steering wheel. "Mind telling

me, exactly, what promise I nonverbally made you?"

He leaned in, sliding my hair over my shoulder. His fingers brushed my bare skin, leaving a trail of goose bumps behind. "The one you made on your knees this morning." His fingers worked down to the roots my hair, giving it the slightest of tugs.

The ragged breath it elicited from me wasn't so slight. "This is your place, Luke. Your home—not some impersonal hotel room. Are you sure you want to do this, be together, like this?"

"I want to be together with you wherever I can be." His fingers curled beneath my chin, tipping it toward him. "But I especially want to be together with you like this tonight."

When my head bobbed, his door flew open.

"Not so fast." I shoved open my door, unlocking the back hatch. "Wheelchair."

His groan echoed through the basement parking garage. "I'm not going to have to stay in the wheelchair for what happens when we get into my apartment, am I?"

"Only if you're lucky." Coming around his side, I patted the back of the wheelchair and waited.

"I'm planning on getting lucky. All night long." His eyes sparked as he crawled out of the SUV into the chair. "Does that count?"

"It counts for something." Locking his SUV, I wheeled him toward the elevator.

I couldn't help the smile that spread on my face—the day had been amazing. Malls and mall food aside, I loved getting to spend time with Luke in such a normal way, meeting his sisters and seeing the roles they played in each other's lives. I adored the stolen glimpses, the private jokes, and the sense of belonging that seemed to come so naturally with the Archer siblings.

They laughed at my jokes, they shared licks of their ice cream cones, and they had no qualms about giving me the same hard time they gave each other. Growing up without siblings and having to split my time between two parents both as a child and now, I hadn't realized how much I'd missed that sense of unity a healthy family had at its core. Even with the Archers losing their parents, the four of them had a strong sense of cohesion I'd never experienced with the closest of family or friends.

"You're thinking," Luke stated once the elevator doors closed us in.

"Why do you say that?"

"Because you're not talking."

"So therefore I must be thinking?"

Luke's shoulder lifted. "That's generally the way it works."

"I'm thinking I just spent more time at the mall today than the sum total of every mall visit of my life, and it's been one of the best days of my life."

"I'm thinking today's been pretty damn great, but it's about to get even better."

"Thank you for sharing today with me, Luke."

His hand wrapped around my wrist. "Thank you for sharing your life with me."

My reaction was to recoil, and I wasn't sure if it was because I was scared of being hurt or hurting him. But I fought my instinct. I fought it until I'd chased it back into the dark, stagnant place it resided.

I fought it until all I could feel was the place where my head and heart came together, the spot where reason and logic lived in harmony with whim and feeling. It was a place I'd never visited before, but experiencing it made me want to take up permanent residence.

Whatever this was, wherever it took me, I wasn't going to hold back. I was all in, to whatever end we found ourselves in.

Feeling that was staggering. Accepting it was freeing. But living it was redefining.

"Still with the thinking," Luke muttered good-naturedly, glancing up at me.

"All done. I'm all thought out."

"Good, because as brilliant as that mind of yours is, I have immediate plans that involve your equally brilliant body." His hand tightened around my wrist when the elevator doors chimed open on his apartment's floor.

"Before you get me behind a locked door, I need you to agree to give me a few minutes before you throw, bend, or spread me over whatever surface you have in your depraved, albeit also brilliant, mind."

Luke pulled his key out when we stopped outside his door. "I'll concede to that. Since I can't get this damn jersey ripped off and in the incinerator fast enough. If you need any more time than I do to strip, I'll wait semi-patiently. Dick in hand. Thinking about dick in you."

Heat spread through my body, originating in the spot between my legs. "Sounds like you've got your whole night planned."

"I *plan* on spending my whole night buried inside you."

"I'll hold you to it."

"And I'll hold you to me while you hold me to it."

"Do you have a comeback for everything I say?" I laughed as he kicked the door open after unlocking it.

"I have a come *on* for everything you say to me. Does that count?"

"Would you care if I said it didn't?"

"No." His head shook.

"Then there's your answer." When I closed the door, the lock sliding over echoed through the quiet space. At the same time it was locking the rest of the world out, it was opening an entire world to me. Before I could change my mind or Luke could change it for me, I rolled him into the living room. "Bathroom?"

"Do you want me to show you where it is?" His mouth took a crooked slant.

"I want you to *tell* me where it is." Snagging my bag hanging off the end of the wheelchair's handholds, I put some space between us.

"Down that hall. First door on the right." Luke watched me back away, a storm of conflict rolling across his face.

"I'll be back. Don't get started without me," I said before turning my back on him.

Luke's chuckle followed me down the hall. "Too late."

That was when I felt the caress of his jersey brush

down my body. Apparently he was serious about not being able to wait another second to have that thing off of him.

Once I was in the bathroom, my hands wouldn't work right. I fumbled my bag, spilling the contents onto the tile floor. At least that made finding what I had in mind that much easier.

After that, my dexterity took another detour from inhibited to inefficient. Trying to peel my dress over my head proved challenging. Unhooking my bra was a damn feat. My panties were easier, but that probably had something to do with gravity's assistance.

Finally, I was naked. Halfway there. Go me for picking the night I felt like my hands had been attacked by a hive of bees as the one when I took the time to wear something special.

Sliding into the item I'd stuffed into my bag earlier, the buttons proved my final challenge before I was set to go. Like Luke, I'd been ready for hours, but being ready was different from getting ready. Now I was both.

Thank god.

I could have taken an extra minute to comb my hair or dab on a little lip gloss, but neither would last. Not to mention my fingers were still in a state of shock.

Opening the door, I stepped into the dark hall. The apartment was quiet. "You didn't fall asleep, did you?"

When it took more than a second for him to answer, I started to worry that he might have.

"No. I'm definitely not asleep." He was standing in the dark living room, totally naked, and totally ready to go.

My heartbeat drummed in my ears. "Good, because I

didn't get all dressed up for nothing." My hands weren't shaking anymore—my fingers no longer fumbling—as they moved to the top button of the jersey to pull it free.

"Seeing you like that almost makes up for what you made me wear all day." His hungry eyes explored me, his shoulder muscles quivering like he was holding himself back.

"Almost?" I moved closer, sliding my finger under the hem of the jersey. "However will I make it up to you?"

Luke scrubbed at his face when I kept teasing the hem of the jersey, sliding it a little higher every few steps. "I've got a few ideas."

I had to fight the smile I felt from seeing him so turned on and growing more impatient with every second I stalled moving closer. When I was only a couple steps away, I stopped. "So do I."

I lifted an eyebrow then gave his hard chest a shove. He fell back onto the couch, landing with a sharp exhale.

"What did I tell you about being on your feet?" Moving between his legs, I stared down at him. Seeing him like this stole the breath from my lungs.

His eyes read a hundred different emotions, his body expressing one—desire. "Does it look like I'm on my feet anymore?"

Shaking my head, I nudged his legs open farther with my knees. They fell open without hesitation.

"You took my feet out from under me, right along with the rest of me." Luke's hands came around the back of my thighs as he stared up at me. "I don't want any of it back either." His finger skimmed around to the front of my thighs and stopped when it reached the bottom button. He worked it free, never breaking his stare. "This is going to make me sound like some lovesick kid, but I don't give a shit." He swallowed and pulled me closer. "Allie, will you be my girlfriend? I know we won't be able to tell anyone, but I don't care. I'll know. You'll know."

He had me in his grasp, ready and willing for the taking, and he was asking me if I'd be his girlfriend? Even when I thought I was starting to figure him out, Luke Archer still surprised the hell out of me.

"Are you asking me to go steady?"

His hands returned to my thighs, disappearing beneath the shirt. "Well, I did already have a secret crush on you, pretend I didn't like you, then I opened with the worst pick-up line ever, so my pride's already gone."

I was smiling from the reminder—at least right until his fingers reached the apex of my legs.

"Will you be my girlfriend?" His knuckles ran over me, his eyes darkening when he felt how ready my body was for his.

"I don't know. Does this mean I get to wear your letterman's jacket?"

Luke leaned his head over the back of the couch, watching me as he touched me, not missing the slightest of gasps or the faintest lowering of my lids. From the way he was studying me, it was almost like he was taking mental notes to refer back to later. "It means you can wear whatever part of me, have whatever piece of me you want."

God, what was happening? Luke Archer was asking me to be his girlfriend like he was some lovesick high school boy at the same time he was touching me in ways no boy would have the first clue about. Before the part of my brain that processed logical thought shut off, I considered my answer. Did I want to be Luke's girlfriend? Did I want an official term? A defined commitment? Did I want to open myself up to the disappointment and heartache that came with a real relationship?

My experience told me I didn't. My future told me I did.

"Honesty," I whispered, sealing my eyes closed as I concentrated on what I needed to say. "I need it. *All* of it. The last serious relationship I had, he ruined me with a lack of honesty. I need to know I can be honest with you and that you are being honest with me."

Luke's fingers pulled back just enough to let my mind work more succinctly. "I'm sorry."

"That's behind me now."

"Are you sure?"

My eyes flew open. "Of course I'm sure. Why?"

Luke's hand found mine. "Because you're bringing it up now. Is your fear of being hurt and betrayed and lied to really in the past? Or is it in the same room with us now, waiting for the chance to come between us?"

My forehead creased as I considered what he was saying. "It's behind me."

Luke nodded. "Good. Because I don't want to pay for some other asshole's mistakes."

Here we were, having serious conversations when we both clearly had sex on our minds. I'd never been asked by a naked god to define a relationship, and I'd never hashed out my insecurities with a man who was so desperate to get laid, the veins running down his neck looked ready to pop.

Nothing about Luke Archer was what it seemed. I loved that about him. It was also what I feared about him.

At the same time I felt like I knew all I needed to know about the man in front of me, I wondered if I'd even scraped the surface. "That's good." I leaned over to splay my hands on his wide chest. "Because I don't want to pay for some bitch's mistakes either."

Luke's chuckle came from low in his chest. "You won't have to. But you do owe me something"—his eyes darted to his rock-hard dick—"and it's time to pay up."

Heat coiled up my body, pulsing between my legs. "Time to make good on my promise."

I lowered onto my knees in front of him, my hands skimming down his chest. When I wound a hand around him, he flinched.

"Fuck, and now I'm about to come like some lovesick kid too." His eyes sealed closed when I glided my hand along him a few times, groaning when my grip tightened.

Fanning my hair over one shoulder, I lowered my head between his legs.

Before my lips could wrap around him, his hands flew to my shoulders, stalling me. "Allie, I didn't mean this . . . I just meant I wanted to have sex with you."

His grip tightened when I blew a warm breath over his skin. "And I'm about to have sex with you." My eyebrow lifted at him. "With my mouth."

His breathing was faster as his hold on my shoulders

loosened. His fingers brushed across my lips. “And what a beautiful mouth it is.”

Letting my head drop between his legs again, I wrapped my hand around his base and parted my lips to take him inside my mouth. A breath hissed from his mouth when I moved down him. His hand fisted in my hair, lightly massaging my head as I struck a slow rhythm.

“Your head between my legs. My name on your back. Coming to this view,” he rasped, starting to pump his hips toward my mouth. “My life could go to shit after this, and I would still die a happy man fifty years from now.”

Chapter Eighteen

I'D SPENT THE night at Luke's. That was the thought I woke with the next morning. More of the night had been filled with love making than actual sleeping, but still, I'd spent the night at his place. I hadn't done that since Ben, the guy who'd taught me what trust was—and what it wasn't.

As I rolled over, I found Luke missing from the bed. Nothing but the dent from his head on his pillow and a few torn condom wrappers on his nightstand to prove he'd been there. Well, and the sting of the red handprint he hadn't been able to resist leaving on my ass last night.

It wasn't quite six yet, but I felt like I could have stayed in bed until lunch. My body was a spent mess. Muscles ached in places I didn't know I had that many muscles to ache. My knees burned from rug burn—for multiple reasons—and the spot between my legs was throbbing from multiple rounds of vigorous sex.

Last night had been about more than sex though.

We'd defined our relationship in no questionable terms. We might not have been able to tell anyone else about it, but we knew, and for me, that was the most important thing. I might have wanted to think I could do open-ended and give-and-take intimacy without commitment, but I couldn't. At least not for long.

Of course a designation didn't come with any guarantees regarding the duration of our relationship. It might last another year, or maybe one more day, but for today, Luke was committed to me and I was committed to him.

For today, that was enough.

Forcing myself out of bed, I grabbed the abandoned jersey from the floor to button it back on. It had lasted through one round of head and Luke bending me over the sofa and taking me that way right after. For as instantly as he'd come both times, I knew his name on my back did more to him than garner a wicked smile.

"Luke?" I called as I padded down the hall.

"Kitchen!" he answered.

As I wandered past the living room, I took in the scene of last night's crimes. It looked like a scene out of *Animal House*—lamps spilled over, clothes hanging from the ceiling fan, more condom wrappers littered around the floor—fitting, since he'd behaved more like an animal than man most of the night.

When I broke into the kitchen, I rolled to a stop when I took in the view. He was standing behind the island, a mess of egg shells and dry pancake mix dusting everything, including his face.

"Damn, that's hot," he said around a whistle as his

eyes roamed me.

"My bedhead?"

"The way you look all freshly fucked and beat from what I did to you last night." His hands braced across the counter, his expression a gloat.

"The male species really never evolved from their cave dweller roots, did they?"

"Other than exchanging grunts for words and clothes for loincloths, no, not really."

I bit at the smile pulling at my mouth, remembering last night—he'd communicated in far more grunts than words—and this morning, he was in nothing more than his loincloth. Or in present day translation—his underwear. Well that, and his Shock ball cap on backward.

"I'd ask if you're hungry, but after what we spent the night doing, I already know your answer." He picked up the spatula and flipped a few pancakes sizzling on a skillet. There was already a foot-high stack of them.

"Luke Archer cooks," I said, trying to make that fit with the image I already had of him.

"With the proper motivation, I've been known to put up a decent meal."

"Proper motivation?"

Luke held out his spatula with a fresh pancake. "Food is calories. Calories are energy." He tore off a piece of pancake and stuffed it into his mouth. "Sex requires energy. So eat up." He slid a plate across the island with a wink.

Pancakes, scrambled eggs, and bacon. My chest tightened. He'd made breakfast for me, but not just any breakfast. My favorite breakfast.

Seeing the food made my stomach grumble loud enough for Luke to hear and say, "Refuel. You're going to need it for what I have planned."

Picking up a piece of bacon from my plate, I waved it at him. "You've got practice this morning, PT this afternoon, and a charity ball tonight. Your schedule is already packed, so you'll have to just make it through the day on the half dozen rounds from last night."

Luke grimaced as I bit into the bacon. "I forgot about the charity ball tonight. Dammit."

"How very charitable of you," I teased.

"If I write a big check, do you think they'd let me out of it?"

I peaked an eyebrow at him. "The main reason most of those people bought one-thousand-dollar tickets was for the privilege of mingling with the San Diego Shock. Since you're kind of the face of the team, I don't think a check of any size will get you out of it."

He glared at the skillet like those pancakes were to blame. Then his face lit up. "Will you go with me?"

"I'm part of the team. I'll already be there."

His head shook. "Will you go *with* me?"

"Oh," I said, looking away. "If I show up with you and hang off your arm all night, won't that kind of ruin our plan of keeping us a secret?"

His shoulders fell. "Maybe?" When I sighed, he added, "Probably. But I don't care. I want you to show up with me, and I want you to hang off my arm all night. We don't need to explain anything to anyone."

"We won't need to if we do that, Luke," I whispered.

"I want to be with you, Allie. Not just behind a locked door. Not just in private. I want to be with you. Seen with you. *With* you, not without you like we'll have to be everywhere we go in public." He dropped the spatula, his hands going to his hips. After a minute of what looked to be deep thought, he sighed. "But I made you a promise. I'll keep this a secret for as long as you want. If that's what it takes to be with you, I'll do it. I might hate every minute of it, but I'll do it."

"I thought you wanted to be discreet about this too?"

"I did, at least until I confirmed that the woman I thought you were is the same one you really are. I know who you are now, and I know I want you. There's nothing discreet about that." Rolling his head a few times, he went back to ladling pancake batter into the skillet. From the size of the batch he'd made, it looked like he was planning on keeping my "energy levels" up into the next decade.

"I love that you feel that way, Luke, I really do." I leaned into the counter as I continued, "But us getting to know each other wasn't the only reason for keeping this quiet."

His jaw tightened for a moment. "I know."

"I've worked hard to get where I am. I've put up with jerks hinting to downright claiming I screwed my way to the top, and if it gets out that I'm screwing Luke Archer, all of the credibility I've worked so hard for will be gone. And I'll never be able to get it back. People will always see me as a joke. As someone who does her best work on her back. I can't let that happen."

He came around the counter and pulled me into his arms. I didn't know I'd been so close to crying until I felt his comfort. "I'd never let that happen." He rubbed circles into my back, holding me with both a strength and gentleness I'd never known. "I'm sorry. I'm just whining. Pouting because I want people to know that you're mine." He kissed the top of my head. "It's the cave dweller ancestry in me."

I laughed quietly against him, letting him soothe me for another minute. "Having you this close is reminding me of that affliction known as morning breath, and since I wasn't planning on spending the night with you, I failed to bring my toothbrush. You might want to keep your distance." Giving him a final squeeze, I wove out of his embrace.

"Lucky for you your 'boyfriend' just so happens to have a stockpile of new toothbrushes."

"A stockpile?" I backed up a few steps because seeing him a few feet in front of me in nothing but his underwear, with that freshly fucked face he was such a fan of, was firing certain desires I should have chased into submission last night back to life.

"Zombie apocalypse planning. You never know when you might need a few dozen new toothbrushes."

"Because who cares if droves of flesh-eating beings are trying to eat your brains? At least you'll have clean teeth."

"See? You get me." He laughed. "That's why I'll share my toothbrushes with you."

"I feel honored." I patted his chest as I moved out of

the kitchen. "Where can I find this toothbrush stockpile?"

"My bathroom. Lower right drawer below the sink."

The way he was looking at me almost made me go back to him, but first, I reminded myself, fresh breath. "Be right back. Save some pancakes for me."

He wandered back over to skillet. "That won't be a problem."

Wandering through his bedroom, I turned into the bathroom. It was clean. *Really* clean. The toilet lid was even down. So he was a caveman with a penchant for cleanliness—I could work with that.

Pulling open the drawer he'd mentioned, I found he really did have a stockpile of toothbrushes. And little toothpastes. And baby bottles of mouthwash. The guy almost had his own travel-sized store of oral hygiene products. Selecting a blue toothbrush, I ripped it open and squeezed a blob of toothpaste on it from the tube resting on the sink.

After giving my teeth an extra good brush, I rinsed and wandered back out into his room with my new toothbrush still in hand. We'd both been a little busy and distracted last night, and I hadn't noticed much more than his body and my proximity to it. I took a minute to explore his room in the light of day.

It was a man's room, hues of gray and blue running throughout. Signed baseballs and wooden bats were propped on shelves, photos of baseball legends scattered in the mix. There was a whole wall of photos of Luke's old teams, from his T-ball team to the Shock. He was easy to spot in each team photo. That smile hadn't changed from the time he was five.

When I got to his dresser on the wall across from his bed, I stopped. At first I thought the photo I was staring at was one of him as a baby. Same big hazel eyes, same honey hair, same smile. It was baby Luke.

But then I noticed what the baby was wearing—a little Shock romper. With the number eleven stitched onto the chest.

My heart stalled for a moment. The Shock had never had a number eleven until Luke Archer joined the ranks three years ago and wanted to keep the number he'd had stamped on his back since he was nine. I'd read the article in the newspaper a while ago, and even though I remembered thinking how silly it was that a grown man would place such an importance on his number, I knew athletes, ball players especially, were superstitious as a breed.

"If you want something to change into, I've got some new clothes in my dresser that should fit you." Luke's voice echoed down the hall before it erupted into the bedroom. "Oh, did you already find them?" he asked when he noticed me in front of his dresser.

"Who's this?"

When Luke's eyes fell on the photo, the skin between his brows creased just enough for me to notice. He didn't say anything at first, letting a storm of emotions thunder across his face.

"Just an old friend's son," he said, looking away.

"An old friend's son you keep a picture of on the dresser in your bedroom . . ."

His shoulders tensed. "If you have a question you

want me to answer, ask it. Otherwise breakfast is getting cold and I've got to get to practice." He waited for me to voice whatever questions he thought I had.

My head was too busy spinning to form any though.

"I'll be in the kitchen," he said quietly, turning to leave.

After Luke left the room, I stood there another minute, studying the baby in the picture. I wouldn't let my assumptions take root. It was a picture of a baby. An old friend's baby. That was it.

Realizing I was still clutching my toothbrush, I headed into the bathroom to drop it off. I paused at the sink, not sure where to put it. There was a toothbrush holder, which seemed like the obvious choice, but it was already holding two toothbrushes. Ignoring the swirl in my stomach wondering why one person had two toothbrushes in their bathroom, I set my toothbrush on the counter, but that didn't look right either.

In the end, I dropped it in the trashcan on my way out.

chapter Nineteen

MY MIND HAD been racing all day. Circling between toothbrushes and trust— baby pictures and trust. *Trust.*

A touchy subject for most people—a volatile one for me.

Deep down, I knew I trusted Luke. It was the surface layer that wondered why I did and if I should. I was at war with myself, no sooner settling the dispute before having it crop up again with renewed vengeance.

Maybe I should have taken a pass on the charity ball. As a member of the support staff, my presence wasn't required. Expected and implied, yes, but I wasn't a player—no one had bought a ticket to rub elbows with the newest athletic trainer on the team.

As soon as I passed through the doors of the ballroom, I knew I shouldn't have come. My head was a mess, and having to be in the same room with him without acknowledging each other as anything more than professional acquaintances was going to be a challenge. For both of us.

The room was already buzzing. Less than an hour into the event, people were milling about the silent auction tables, sipping champagne, and huddling around the Shock players.

I wasn't looking for him, at least not exactly, but it was almost like I knew right where he was. The crowd of people clustered around him may have helped with his location. Or maybe it had more to do with the way he was already looking at me when I found him.

Our eyes locked, and the room revolved around me. Number eleven in his baseball uniform at the end of a hard-won game was the sexiest thing in the world—but Luke Archer in a tux was a close second.

He was the first to tame his stare, but I stood in place for another minute, reeling. I wasn't trying to look at him, but I couldn't seem to help it. Especially with the frequent looks he kept sending in my direction. We were fools to think we could be around each other like this without being together.

In an effort to ease the mounting tension, I wandered to the far side of the room, away from him. It didn't seem to help with the looks, but at least I couldn't make out his laugh or voice from this distance.

A few members of the medical staff waved at me as I milled through the room in search of a drink, but most were there with their spouses or significant others. A few days at home were not to be wasted when we spent as much time on the road as we did. Everyone had someone it felt like—Luke Archer had the whole damn room—except for me.

I had no one. Self-pity. It wasn't a position I liked to find myself in, and if I couldn't chase it away with force of will, I'd try chasing it away with something stronger.

The first glass of champagne went down in two swallows. The second one I was just finishing when someone also on their own wandered up to the bar beside me. Noting my vanishing drink, Shepherd lifted two fingers at the bartender.

"I'm here for the free booze too." Shepherd held out a glass for me, waiting.

"I'm not here for the free booze," I replied before draining what was left in my second glass before accepting the fresh glass from him.

A smirk settled on his face. "No? Then what are you here for? Because Uncle Sam knows neither of us make enough to put a down payment on the items being auctioned off tonight to benefit some country that's going to be renamed and run by some other dickface in a year."

Shepherd wasn't my favorite person to be around. Actually, he might have been one of my least favorite, but as the crowd around Archer continued to grow, Shepherd's company became more desirable. I'd rather be talking to him than no one.

"I'm here to support the team," I said right before I hiccupped. The champagne had gone straight to my head, which was a welcome relief since alcohol was clouding my Luke Archer Rubik's cube of confusion.

"And support the team you do." Shepherd followed

where my gaze had moved to. That same person stationed in the center of the room, holding a room full of people in his hand. "So very, very well."

"What does that mean?" My eyes narrowed from his tone or from what he was alluding to with his tone.

"This is Archer's best season. And it's not like his three prior seasons were shit, if you know what I mean."

"I'm sure I don't have a clue."

"All I'm saying is that whatever you're doing, keep it up, Allie." Shepherd slid a little closer, his gaze dropping to where the V in my dress came together. "Archer stays this hot, I see a World Series win in our future."

The skin on the back of my neck tingled. From what he was saying, from how he was saying it, from the way he was looking at me. I wanted to play dumb and deny his veiled accusation, but I hadn't approached anything in life by playing dumb and I wasn't about to start with the likes of Shepherd.

"Whatever you're trying to say, Shepherd, spit it the hell out. My head's swimming in too much champagne to figure out cryptic riddles."

Shepherd didn't stop running his eyes over me, and with him getting closer, I could make out the glassiness in his eyes. He was marinating in more champagne than I was.

"I'm saying that of all the Incentive Girls I've seen thrown at Archer, you're the one who's squeezed the best results out of our boy. Or should I say fucked the best results out of him." Shepherd's head tipped, his smile eclipsing into one that made me shiver.

"You're drunk."

"And you must be such a slut in bed, you might actually get to hang around for a second season. Most of the girls the team brings on only last a year, but you"—he whistled, shaking his head—"you just might be this generation's Marilyn."

Setting my glass down, I put some space between us. "At this point in your depravity, I think it's a good thing I have no idea what you're talking about."

"Oh, please. Marilyn Monroe? Joe DiMaggio? Why do you think he became the legend he is today?"

"Oh, I don't know. Because he was a great ball player?"

"Made great because he got to look forward to a fine piece of ass crawling over his cock every night."

His words hit me like someone had just slapped me across the cheek. Whatever sexual harassment policies the team had drawn up, Shepherd was breaking just about every single one of them.

"You are an asshole."

"Oh, please. That woman couldn't act to save her soul. But servicing dick—she could have taken home the Academy Award."

Anger coursed through me, mixing with the alcohol. It was a volatile combination. "I wasn't calling you an asshole because of what you're accusing Marilyn Monroe of. I was and still am calling you an asshole because of what you're accusing me of." Nevermind the fact that DiMaggio and Monroe hadn't even met until after he'd retired from baseball. Clearly, Shepherd wasn't up on his baseball trivia like I was.

Shepherd exchanged his empty glass for the one I'd left unfinished on the counter. "What? Are you *not* servicing Luke Archer's dick?"

My stomach turned over. How did he know? How had he found out?

"Don't worry, Allie. Your valiant Archer didn't fuck and tell or anything." He drained my glass in a single sip. "It was just implied in your contract when you were brought on."

"I was brought on as an athletic trainer. Athletic trainer. The same exact job as the one you have." When I realized my hands were starting to shake, I wound them behind my back. I didn't want him to see me rattled. I didn't want to confirm his suspicions.

"Yes, you were brought on as an 'athletic trainer.'" He snorted. "Just like the girl last season was brought on as a 'physical therapist,' and the one before her as a 'dietitian,' and the one Archer's first season as a 'guest reporter.'"

The room started to close in on me. I had no reason to believe what Shepherd was saying; just like I had no reason to disbelieve what he was saying. He might have been an asshole, but he was a drunk one right now and couldn't have just pulled all of that out of his ass if it wasn't true. Or could he?

God, my head hurt.

"Oh please, don't be so naïve." Shepherd dropped his hand on my shoulder and gave me a little shake like he was trying to break me out of shock. "How do you think a team attracts a player like Archer and *keeps* a player like him? It sure as shit isn't with just heaps of cash. But it's not exactly like the Shock can put a traveling hooker on the payroll, so they've found legal ways around it."

I shrugged out from beneath his hand, my eyes searching the room for Archer. He was still in the same place, but he was watching me. When he noticed the look on my face, his brows drew together. His eyes narrowed when he saw Shepherd so close.

It wasn't true. It couldn't be. Whatever I did or didn't know about Luke, I knew he was a decent person. A good man. Someone like that wouldn't condone or expect the team to hire some new woman every year to be his personal traveling fuck toy. Shepherd was full of shit.

"God, what is the matter with you?" Peeling my eyes from Archer, who looked close to tearing across the room for me, I crossed my arms at Shepherd. "Are you intimidated by me or something? Worried I'm going to take your position as lead trainer?"

His head fell back, and a laugh spilled past his lips. "Oh, yeah. That's it. I'm truly intimidated by your ability to use your pussy." My eyes widened, but he didn't notice or didn't care. "Please, what did you really think? That you were hired on because you were the best candidate for the job? This is baseball. It's a boys' club. The only cunts allowed in are the ones who know how to spread 'em and bed 'em."

At my side, my hand twitched. The pull to slap him right in the middle of this charity ball was so appealing, I could taste it, but Luke was watching me again. I couldn't give him a reason to come barreling over here and confirm Shepherd's accusations. "You truly are a heinous person."

Shepherd feigned insult. "You misunderstand why I'm bringing this up. It isn't to insult you—it's to congratulate you." He clapped a few times at me. "You've done your job better than any of the ones who came before. Keep up the good work. Who knows? You might even get a little bonus at the end of the season—with your marching orders."

I didn't realize I'd been backing away from him until he cocked his brow at me. I was not going to be intimidated by someone like Shepherd. I was not going to let him think he could fire off some random threats and I'd lose all manner of composure and decorum.

"The wires in your head? Uncross them. Or exorcise the demon you've been possessed by. Or have your meds adjusted. And don't talk to me again unless it's about something work related." I didn't blink as I spoke, moving closer with every word and making sure he saw the seriousness on my face. I turned to leave once that slapping urge took me over again.

"Has he told you about the little boy yet?" Shepherd's voice carried after me. "The one Incentive Girl Number One got knocked up with his first season?"

My feet froze in the middle of my next step. My heart froze with it.

Chapter Twenty

AFTER THE BALL, I went home and got drunk like I'd never gotten drunk before. I shut off my phone, turned off the lights, and drank my way through the neck and shoulders of a nice bottle of bourbon.

It seemed like a good idea at the time. The next morning made me question if it wasn't the worst idea instead.

My phone I kept off, knowing what would happen when I powered it back on and found all of his missed calls and texts. I'd call him back. I'd let him explain what Shepherd had said. I'd let his explanation cloud my reason. I'd let myself become the very person I was afraid of becoming again—the girl who exchanged what she wanted to be true for the actual truth.

The team was scheduled to fly out later that afternoon, and I was dreading the flight. Not just because I'd have to see Archer, but I'd have to face Shepherd again too. Have to face the whole team. How many of them thought the same thing Shepherd did—that I was just number eleven's new fuck girl?

After downing a few aspirins and a few liters of water to rehydrate myself, I slid in front of my laptop and got to work. My apartment got good light early in the day, but I had to close the blinds to keep my head from splitting open. Plus, the dark fit my mood, given the content of my research.

Type Luke Archer's name into a search engine and thousands of pages of baseball related pictures and stats would pop up. That wasn't what I was searching for. Type "Luke Archer's love interests" into the same search engine, and the whole tone of the pictures and articles changed.

From high school dance photos to candid snapshots taken at college parties with some girl he was caught talking with, the photos made him seem like some playboy who had had a different girl for every night of his existence since puberty. The propaganda wasn't what I was interested in either though.

Adjusting my search, I found what I was looking for—the guest reporter who'd followed the Shock three seasons ago. Her name was Callie Monahan, and at the time, she'd been a reporter for a big national station. She was about my age, had gone to a good school, and had seemed to be rising in her career, but for the past few years, there wasn't much of anything about her. She didn't work for the same national station—or any station for that matter.

I couldn't find any direct links between her and Luke—at least, not at first. It wasn't until I was scrolling through some of the images of Callie that I found one that made my body go numb. It was a photo some fan had taken at a team dinner. Everyone from Coach to the players to the support staff to the guest reporter was in it.

Luke and Callie weren't sitting by each other. They weren't even sitting on the same side of the table. It wasn't their proximity to one another that told me what I needed to know—it was how clearly aware they both were of where the other one was. While everyone else was looking at the camera, Luke and Callie were looking at each other. It had probably only been a fraction of a moment, but it had been frozen in time and made public for anyone to see.

The wheels of my computer chair rolled closer as I leaned in to study the photo. My ears were ringing like I'd just been knocked over the head with a brick. It wasn't just that the two of them were looking at each other; it was the way he was looking at her. It was familiar. Achingly familiar. The set of his brow, the tip of his smile, the intensity in his eyes—it was the way Luke looked at me.

It was the same way he'd looked at her.

Jealousy was taking root, but I didn't let it grow. Luke had a right to a past. He had a right to look at some other woman with care and concern. He had history with this woman, but that wasn't why I was taped to my laptop when I could have used the extra hour of sleep. The women in his past weren't what concerned me—it was how they'd become a part of his life.

I needed to see if Shepherd's story had any credibility, because if it did, what did that say about why I'd been hired, why Luke had come into my life, and what the future of my career looked like?

I guessed I knew what it would say—I just wasn't sure I was ready to hear it.

Scrolling through the last images of Callie, I couldn't find any of her and Luke together. They'd been careful, just as we'd been. But in the last few images, I found yet another familiar face. This one was familiar because of the photo propped on Luke's dresser.

It was the same baby in Callie's arms, taken at about the same time as Luke's photo, judging by the age of the baby. The caption read nothing more than "Callie Monahan and son," but I knew.

He wasn't just her son. With those eyes and that mouth, I knew who the father was.

My chest started heaving from my breathing. Why hadn't he told me? Why would Luke keep something so big from the woman he was seeing . . . unless he had no intention of "seeing" her past the expiration of the season? Unless seeing was code word for using. Girlfriend code word for fuck toy.

My fingers curled into the armrests of the chair. I'd seen enough—I should just let this settle in before I went any further down this vortex. Before I could control what was happening, I typed something else into the search engine. Something about the Shock's team dietician two seasons ago.

That hole in my stomach stretched wider. Another young woman who'd only stayed a season.

My fingers flew across the keyboard again. Typing in Shock's physical therapy team for the season last year, I scrolled through the images until I found the one I was searching for. Same exact thing. Young woman. One season.

For a minute I just stared at her picture, shock rendering me motionless. When the shock receded just enough to let comprehension in, I noticed something.

She had blond hair, brown eyes, and was on the petite side. Scanning back to the team dietician, same story. I didn't need to go back to Callie's photos to confirm the same thing.

Luke Archer had a type, and it seemed the team had been catering to his preferences ever since he'd signed on. He had a type. Blond, brown-eyed, petite, and willing to crawl into bed with him.

That was when the room began to spin again, though it wasn't from the alcohol—it was from a harsh dose of reality setting in. The Shock hadn't hired me on merit and talent alone, like I'd believed. They hadn't hired the three women before me on any of that either.

I'd been brought on for one reason and one reason only—to keep Luke Archer happy and swinging for the fences. Blood rolled to a boil in my veins, anger masking the pain.

He was about to get a dose of harsh reality himself.

Chapter Twenty-One

CLIMBING ABOARD THE team plane that afternoon took every ounce of courage I had at my disposal. I'd talked myself into resigning mid-season a hundred times already—and I'd talked myself out of it a hundred times. Despite feeling like a joke being here, I knew to up and leave in the middle of a team's season would look bad. Any hopes I had for continuing my career in professional sports would be dashed. I didn't want one season to define the rest of my career, so I told myself to suck it up and finish the season strong. I reminded myself that these kinds of trials were what made people stronger and that by the end of this, I would be made of steel.

Convincing myself to finish the season was easy. Or, easier. Convincing myself that I didn't have feelings for Luke Archer was not. It should have been. After everything I'd learned in the past twenty-four hours, accepting that anything I had or did feel for him had all been based on a giant ruse should have been simple.

It wasn't though. When I thought about Luke, I still felt things for him. I still felt my stomach tighten when I thought of the way he looked at me. I still felt that surge of hope for when I'd get to see him next. I still felt that sense of peace and belonging when I thought about him.

I hated myself for all of it. I despised myself for still caring about some man who'd lied to me and betrayed me. That was okay though, I convinced myself, because I could make hate work. Hate kept the fire of anger burning—I would have been in more trouble if I'd forgiven myself for my weakness.

As I stepped inside the cabin, I'd never been so aware of my expression and making sure the one I'd practiced in the mirror earlier stayed in place. Most of the team was already on board, buckled into their seats with their headphones on. Some of them already looked asleep, some were looking at the windows, and some were playing on their phones. But one was looking up, straight at me.

My lungs strained when I felt his stare on me. He didn't know I knew. He was still looking at me like I meant something—like I was special. He was good at that. I supposed he had to be. None of us had known why we'd been hired—not the real reason. It wasn't like he could just be an ass and we'd beg him to fuck us sideways all season. Luke had to look at us like that. He had to make each of us feel special. He had to do that so we would all give him what he wanted without making it seem like some carefully crafted plan built to keep the star player happy and the team wins adding up.

Giving him the most passing glance I was capable of,

I kept moving by his row. I didn't miss the way he indicated the window seat empty beside him. I didn't miss the damn tiny box with a bow on it resting on the empty seat.

I felt like someone was ripping my heart to pieces when I passed him. I could hear him twisting around in his seat, watching me. I could feel his stare as I wound farther down the aisle, putting me as far away from him as the plane would allow.

Just when I was about to take the empty row at the back of the plane, I changed my mind. Knowing Luke, once the plane was in the air, he'd come back to sit with me, and I wasn't ready to talk to him. I'd have to soon, but not yet. The sting of it all was too fresh. I knew I'd say things I'd regret.

"Mind if I squeeze in beside you?" I stopped outside of the row Reynolds was stretched out in.

He slid off his big headphones, confusion forming on his face. "Be my guest, Doc." He motioned at the empty seat beside him and stood to let me squeeze by.

The whole time, I felt Archer watching. As I turned to sit, our gazes met for just long enough I could see the same lines of confusion drawn on his forehead. To distract myself, I fought with the buckle, trying to get it adjusted to fit me, but being flustered and nervous was making basic things difficult.

"Do you need some help?" Reynolds asked.

"I've got it."

"Sure about that?" he said when I started beating the two ends together when they refused to latch.

A moment later, I got them to cooperate. "I've got it,"

I breathed, sagging into the seat.

A few minutes passed in silence except for my shifting every few seconds, trying to get comfortable. I was having a difficult time deciding if I wanted the window shade open or closed.

By the time we were in the air and I was still a shifting, undecided wreck, Reynolds leaned over. "Do you need to talk, Doc?"

Finally I found the right position I felt comfortable in, settling on the window being closed. "No," I said, closing my eyes. "I need to forget."

Chapter Twenty-Two

I'D SURVIVED THE plane. I'd survived the walk through the airport, when he'd tried coming up beside me and slipping something into my hand, by dodging into the women's bathroom before he could get the little box in my grip. I'd survived the drive to the hotel. I'd survived the awkward moments when he'd tried to get my attention and I'd pretended not to notice. I'd survived the day.

I wasn't sure I'd survive the night. I wasn't sure I'd survive the hotel.

As soon as the team had gotten checked in, I'd disappeared into my room and hadn't left it. The phone started ringing five minutes after I locked myself inside. Since my cell was still turned off, I guessed he figured he'd try to get a hold of me this way. After the third call went unanswered, I took the phone off the hook. I wasn't ready.

My cell I turned back on because I couldn't risk missing a team call, but I kept it on silent so his calls, which came in every fifteen minutes, wouldn't echo through the room. I refused to look at the stream of texts coming in from him, or the ones I'd missed.

As a distraction, I flipped the television on to break the silence and the tone of my thoughts. It didn't work.

It was just past eleven when a soft knock sounded outside my door. I'd just been heading into the bathroom when I froze. It wasn't housekeeping on the other side.

"Allie?" His voice was quiet, but it seemed to echo through my room like a shout. "I know you're in there. I heard you moving around. I've been standing outside of your room for ten minutes trying to figure out what the hell to say. Trying to figure out what the hell's going on. Are you okay?" A thud came from the other side of the door, like he'd dropped his forehead into it. "Are *we* okay?"

When I didn't reply in the form of words or opening the door, I heard him sigh. "Is this about the charity ball the other night? Are you upset about something I did? Mad that we didn't go together? Because you know how I feel about that. I don't care if people see us. I don't care if everyone finds out we're together. I'm tired of pretending."

His words were so sincere, the ache in them so raw. My throat was burning from the emotions erupting inside me. It was unfair that the world had created a man who could master such sincerity when none existed beyond the façade.

"Please talk to me. Please just open the door. Scream at me. Slap me. Just do something. This silent thing is killing me, Allie. This isn't how two people communicate." Another thud on the outside of the door. "Please just tell me what you're upset about so I have the opportunity to explain myself or share my side of the story. I can't fix this if I don't know what's wrong."

My arms crossed like I was trying to keep myself together. There was nothing to fix, because there'd been nothing between us. You can't fix something you never had.

"Allie? Please?" His voice was louder now, tight with emotion.

That was when I almost caved. That was when my body angled toward the door, my hand lifting in its direction. That was when I realized how weak I'd become because of him. I could barely control my own body. I was incapable of controlling my own thoughts, he'd rendered me into such a fragile state. The strength I'd known had left me in my most desperate moment, and part of me hated him for that.

I should have known what I'd felt for him wasn't the real thing. I should have known it was false, because weren't the people we cared for supposed to make us stronger instead of weaker? Weren't they supposed to make us steadfast instead of feeble?

"I'm sliding a note under your door with a place and a time tomorrow morning. I'll be there waiting. You can make me wait all day if you want, just please show up eventually. Please tell me what's wrong so I can make it right."

When a folded up piece of paper slipped under my door, I flinched, but I didn't move. He was still waiting outside the door. I wondered if he'd wait there all night.

"For whatever I did, or for whatever you think I did, I'm sorry."

His footsteps moved away from my door, but it wasn't until I heard the elevator doors ping that I felt safe to move. I could have left his note on the carpet, but I knew I wouldn't be able to fall asleep with it sitting in plain view. After grabbing it, I rushed into the bathroom and was about to drop it in the garbage can when I thought twice. If I woke up in a moment of weakness, I could grab it and read what he'd written. In another moment of weakness, I could actually show up to wherever he was planning on being in the morning. In the worst moment of weakness possible, I could let him construct a story and an explanation I'd buy until I was reminded of the reality of it when the season ended, taking my employment with the team with it.

Veering toward the toilet, I dropped the letter inside and flushed it before I could change my mind. I tried not to let the irony of that letter's journey hit me.

THE INEVITABLE. I couldn't put it off another minute longer. After failing to sleep last night and spending the rest of the day hiding in my room, I was done. I was done feeling weak and acting like it. We were both employees of the Shock, and it wasn't like I could reasonably avoid him the next two months of the season.

Confrontation. I'd have to do it eventually, and I guessed as soon as I stepped foot in that locker room, it would happen. That was fine. If he wanted to so desperately know why I'd cut him off, I'd let him know. He was an idiot if he didn't already have an idea why.

Instead of taking the bus the team had chartered over to the stadium, I let Coach know I'd catch a cab over. Shepherd was technically who I reported to, but after our last conversation, which was about as unprofessional as it got, I wasn't eager to report anything to him. Least of all why I was taking a cab instead of the team bus, because he'd know why. He'd love knowing why. I couldn't deal with Shepherd's gloating today. Not with everything else.

The locker room was buzzing when I shoved through the doors. After the win of the home game and the season continuing to go so well, the guys were almost acting like they'd already bagged the pennant. Tonight's game against the New York Vikings should be a straightforward win. The players knew it too.

Shit-eating grins and Viking jokes were flying around the room. The only holdout was one player sitting on the bench in front of his locker, his head cast down, the only one who hadn't changed into his uniform.

His back was to me, and I had every intention of getting straight to work, but seeing him like that hit me hard. I'd seen Archer after the two losses the team had taken this season, and he hadn't looked a fraction as distraught as he did now.

A ball lodged in my throat out of nowhere. I wondered how long he'd waited this morning. I wondered what he'd thought with every minute that passed when I didn't show up. I wondered what he'd looked like when he left. I wondered about it all when really, I shouldn't have been wondering about any of it.

As though he could sense my presence or the tone of my thoughts, his back stiffened right before his head rotated over his shoulder. Our eyes locked, and while I was trying to fake the indifference in mine, the hurt in his was the genuine thing.

Shoving to a stand, he turned toward me, making no qualms about where he was heading as he moved through the locker room. The look on his face, the way he was moving toward me, I knew I had to get out of there. From the set of his jaw, I guessed he didn't care if the whole locker room heard what he was about to say.

Veering to the right, I ducked into the med room. Just as I was closing the door, it shoved open.

"You're not shutting this door on me too." Archer moved inside the room, closed the door, and pressed the lock.

If this was the way he wanted to do this, then fine. No time would be opportune for confronting him. Slipping an imaginary coat of armor into place, I crossed my arms at him. "Looks like you didn't exactly wait all day for me to show up."

He had to work his jaw loose to respond. "After six hours, I got the hint that you weren't planning on showing up."

He'd waited six hours. I didn't know why, but at the same time I felt myself harden with guilt, I softened with affection. Both were erased by the anger that surged to the surface when I realized I was letting emotions cloud my judgment where Luke Archer was concerned.

"Six hours isn't all day. Try not to make a habit of lying—you might get caught in one someday."

"You're pissed at me. At least I know that now." He motioned at me, his voice annoyingly calm. "What would be really helpful to know is *why* you're pissed at me?"

My teeth sank into my tongue to keep from lashing out my answer. The honest one. "I'm not pissed at you, Luke. I'm just over you."

He made a face. "What does that mean?"

"This. Us." I waved my finger between him and me. "I'm done. I'm out. Over it."

He was about to snap something back when he caught himself. Scrubbing his face, he took a few breaths before opening his mouth. "And you decided this when?"

My shoulder lifted. "A little while ago."

"You said yes to wearing my letterman jacket three nights ago, Allie. What in the hell's changed since then?"

Besides finding out why I'm really here? "Oh, please, Luke. You and I both knew this wouldn't go anywhere. It was fun, but it's time to move on."

"'It was fun'? Is that really all you saw us as? Is that really all you wanted?"

"What did you want? You were the one trying to get me into bed two sentences after introducing yourself to me. What did you really want if it wasn't a lot of no-commitment-required fucking?"

My words hit him like a shove. Backing into the door, his body hit it with a heavy thud. "Is that what you really think? That all I wanted was a few good fucks out of you?" He waited for my answer but kept going when I didn't give him one. I didn't feel the need to provide a verbal confirmation. "Maybe I shouldn't have come on so strong, maybe I shouldn't have fallen into bed with you so quickly." When I exhaled sharply, he kicked his heel against the door. "Okay, I *know* now I shouldn't have, but I pursued you not because I wanted to get between your legs but because I was hoping to work my way, eventually, into your heart."

I didn't know I'd grabbed one of the folded towels on the counter beside me before it was flying at his face.

"What the hell, Allie?" Archer ducked the first one, but he didn't move when I threw the next few. He let them hit him, one right after the next, until I'd gone through the whole pile.

I didn't feel any better after. That he could stand there and say those things and seem so sincere and be so full of shit wasn't fair.

"Just give it up, Archer. It's fine. We're both adults. Consenting ones." I hoped the tremor in my voice was only noticeable to me. "But it's run its course."

"Why are you saying this?"

"Because it's the truth. You can call it what you want, but our relationship was based on sex. You don't need to apologize. It was great; I just need to move on now."

His shoulders tensed. "It was not based on sex."

"It was. It was about two reproductive organs that really liked each other. Don't make it something it wasn't."

The emotion he'd managed to hold back was pouring out of him now, filling the room. "*Isn't*," he snarled. "Stop talking about us like we're in the past."

My throat burned, but I kept saying what I needed to. "That's what history is, Luke. The past."

His arms wound around the back of his head as he shoved off from the door. He looked lost, the way a person might when they woke up from a coma. "Please tell me what's wrong."

"Nothing's wrong." I chewed on my cheek. "There's nothing to fix or explain or apologize for. I enjoyed my time with you, but it's over."

His eyes narrowed on me. "Oh, please. You are no more the person who looks for no-strings relationships than I am."

I bit back the *bullshit* that found its way to my lips and reminded myself to stay cool. To play it off like emotions hadn't been involved. "You barely know me. How can you say that?"

"I know plenty."

Yeah, you knew all you needed to know to meet your needs. "Well, if you did, you'd know I was just like every other woman who couldn't pass up the opportunity to be bedded by Luke Archer." I smiled sweetly at him while bitterness churned in my stomach. "I mean, come on, who wouldn't want to brag to their friends about scoring with the Homerun King?"

Hurt spread across his face, settling into his eyes. Just when I thought he was going to turn around and leave, he powered across the room toward me. He backed me into the wall, but not by touching me. The look on his face was enough to move me until I could go no farther. He lowered his head until he was at my eye level. Then he waited for my eyes to meet his.

"It's going to take a hell of a lot more than that to push me away," he said, leaning in so close I could feel the warmth of his breath. "A hell of a lot more."

He gave that a moment to set in before he stormed for the door. With his hand on the handle, he paused. "Oh, and by the way, my leg's doing great. You know, in case my athletic trainer was concerned."

I stayed planted by the wall, steeling myself. "If you're still having problems with it, run it by Shepherd. You two seem to be better suited for each other."

THE SHOCK LOST the game. A game they were favored by a large margin to win. The top team in the nation had just had their asses handed to them by one of the lowest-ranked teams in professional baseball.

That loss might have had a lot to do with a certain clutch hitter striking out three times, getting walked twice, and getting out before he'd made it to first base the one time his bat did manage to connect with the ball.

Number eleven hadn't just had an off night—he'd had the kind of night people would be talking about for years. He'd errored more times in this one game than he had in his entire career. He'd moved like he'd just had a hip replaced and the surgeon had gone ahead and replaced his shoulder too.

It wasn't just Archer who'd been off tonight though—the entire team had. Even though the Shock wasn't just Luke Archer, in a lot of ways, Luke Archer was the spirit of the Shock. He led the team to victories by example, but tonight, the only example he'd set was one of listlessness.

After Coach had screamed his lungs out after the game, we all left that locker room in a state of shock. *What the hell had just happened?* was written on all of our expressions.

It was the same question I was asking myself as I rode the elevator to my hotel room. The team would be rolling out bright and early for the next game, and after last night's state of no sleep, I was eager to crawl into bed and punch erase on this day of horrors.

Like earlier, I'd elected to take a cab back instead of the team bus, explaining I had a few things to wrap up before leaving. After Archer's and my talk before the game, he hadn't said a word to me. He hadn't so much as looked my way, not even when he crawled back into the dugout after each strike out and I held out a bottle of water for him. Maybe what I'd said had finally set in. Maybe he was already over me.

Maybe he was already having someone line up his next Incentive Girl since this season's had cut him off early. I didn't have the first clue why he'd gone from seeming like he'd cross an ocean on a paddleboard to keep from losing me to acting like I didn't exist.

When the elevator doors opened, I stuck my head out to make sure he wasn't waiting outside my door as I was half-expecting he might be. When I felt a stab of disappointment because he wasn't there, I made myself remember what Shepherd had told me.

Disappointment was a distant memory by the time I shoved open my door.

My room was not the way I'd left it. It didn't even look like my room at all. The bags hanging over my shoulder fell to the floor, my mouth dropping open as I took in the room. On every surface that was solid or firm enough to support a vase, a bouquet of flowers had made its way onto it. But there wasn't just one bouquet per surface—there were as many as could fit on that surface.

At least four on each nightstand, a dozen lining the window ledge, I couldn't count how many on the desk . . . they were everywhere. Even in the bathroom, I discovered when I checked. Vases were scattered along the floor, petals strewn across the bed, overwhelming and beautiful by every definition of the terms.

A hundred varieties of flowers made up the bouquets bursting with color, creating a scent that was just as sweet as it was floral. It was the grandest gesture I'd ever had done for me. The grandest by far.

I didn't need to open the note propped on my bed to know who was responsible for this. I shouldn't have, because flowers or not, it didn't change anything.

I couldn't help it though. Lifting the card, I found only one simple sentence scratched down in his handwriting.

You're more.

My eyes kept moving over the words, almost like they were trying to convince themselves there was some other message I was missing. There wasn't though.

What did that mean? "You're more"? More than what? More than a fling? More than the girls before me?

More of a pain in the ass? Or more than something else I had yet to discover?

You're more.

Those words haunted me all night, but by the next morning, I'd realized that words were just words. It was the actions behind them that gave them their meaning.

Archer's actions did not support his words. These two on the note or the ones he'd uttered in the med room before the game yesterday.

You're more. Whatever he meant by it, it was just a ploy to keep me on his string for the next couple of months. A damage control measure.

No more. That was my response.

chapter Twenty-Four

ANOTHER CITY. ANOTHER game. Another disaster.

We were at the top of the ninth, and unless one of those miracle things decided to fall from the sky, the Shock was adding another loss to their season.

The team's spirit had been sullen from the start and it had only gone down from there. Coach looked close to exploding as he paced the dugout like a wounded lion, cursing under his breath about replacing the entire lot of babies for some real players.

The team didn't function without every player giving it their all. Especially when that player was Luke Archer. He'd been a mess during the game in New York—he'd been worse in this one. Only a couple of days had gone by since our talk, but to look at him, it was like he'd been marooned on a deserted island for months. His face was unshaven, his eyes sunken, his expression hardened.

I'd done my best to avoid him, but he'd done his best to thwart my plans. He never said anything—he just locked his eyes on mine for a moment—but that said everything he was trying to get across.

He wanted to talk. But there was nothing to talk about. I didn't want to bring up what I'd found out from Shepherd because part of me had too much pride to admit that that was the reason I'd called it off. I wanted to be the first girl to cut him off before he got the chance. I wanted him to think I was done because I was done, not because of what I'd found out. I wanted to walk away with as much dignity as I could, because I didn't feel like I had much.

I'd lost him. I was going to lose my job. I was close to losing my credibility.

I'd lost enough without adding in the last remnants of my pride.

"Hey, Allie, what gives?" Shepherd stopped in front of where I was settled on the bench. "Archer isn't looking good out there. Might need to pull a late night. Make sure he's all set to go for the next game."

It was faint, but I didn't miss the wink he gave me before wandering down to the other end of the dugout. My fists curled in so tightly, I could feel my nails close to drawing blood from my palms. The only perk to getting let go from my dream job at the end of the season would be not having to deal with Shepherd anymore.

"How's it hangin', Doc?" Reynolds crashed into the seat beside me, nudging me not-so-lightly. When he saw the look on my face, he snorted. "Sorry about that. Force of habit. How are you doing?" he corrected, trying to sound as eloquent as a big guy from Alabama could.

"I'm okay."

Reynolds nodded, his eyes drifting toward the Shock player stepping up to the plate. “You know who isn’t okay?”

My shoulders fell when I saw Luke. His routine of tapping his cleats and eyeing the spot on the fence he wanted to sail the ball over had been replaced by slouching up to the plate with an expression that embodied withdrawn.

“Yeah, he’s had a rough game.” I had to look away. I’d spent enough time wondering if I was making the right decision just cutting him off without so much as having a conversation like a couple of adults.

“That’s not the okay I was talking about.” Reynolds threw me another not-so-gentle nudge. “What’s going on with you two?”

I glanced at him from the side. He met me with a raised brow. Fantastic. So the players were in on the secret too.

“Nothing’s going on with us two.”

“Yeah? Is that why you can’t look at him without looking like you’re either about to cry or curse?”

When a collective groan echoed through the dugout, I sighed. *Strike one*.

“Did he tell you?” I asked.

“Didn’t have to.” When I twisted in my seat to see what he meant, he added, “I could tell. I could see it when he looked at you. I could hear it when he talked about you.”

I held my breath as the pitcher wound up. “Did you know about the arrangement?”

"What arrangement?" He cursed when Archer's bat swung around, connecting with air. *Strike two*. "Are you two 'arranged' to be married or something?" When he moved to nudge me again, I slid down the bench a little to ease the impact. "What arrangement?"

Reynolds didn't know. Probably none of the players did, I thought. It wouldn't go over well that the team had set aside a special someone for one player but none for the rest of them.

"Never mind." My tone came out too biting. Reynolds didn't miss it.

"Listen, Doc, if Archer did something to hurt you, I know it wasn't on purpose."

My hands curled around the front of the bench as the pitcher stared Archer down with smugness on his face—two strikes, zero balls. We all knew where this was likely going.

"I know he might seem kind of distant at first, removed when you meet him, but it's because he's Luke Archer. He's careful because women look at him and see a windfall." Reynolds leaned forward on the bench with the rest of the players as the pitcher wound up again. "Just do him right, okay? He's been done wrong before. He's one of the good ones."

I was saved my response when the pitcher threw his third pitch. Archer's bat moved like he was swinging through rock instead of air. The ball hissed into the catcher's glove.

Strike three.

THE TEAM BUS was silent after the game. Other than the rumble of the engine and the whir of air conditioning, the loss had taken the words right out of the team.

I'd managed to avoid Luke in the locker room, busy tending to other players who needed to be taped and stretched, but every once in a while, I felt him watching me. It was a strange feeling and one I'd never felt before. It felt like someone was tapping on my shoulder, trying to get my attention, but when I turned around, no one was there. Like my mind had made up the whole thing, and then I'd find Luke watching me with that same look I'd seen a lot the past few days—like he was trying to figure out a way to save something that couldn't be saved.

As was my new habit, I'd slid into the seat beside Reynolds for the ride back to the hotel. He looked like he was asleep, so I wouldn't have to worry about him harassing me about Luke again.

The bus had just pulled away from the Pioneers' stadium when I noticed someone coming down the aisle toward us. With the way Luke was looking at me, it was no mystery where he was heading.

In a bus packed with people, it wasn't like he could just stand in the aisle and have it out with me, and thankfully I had Reynolds taking up the seat beside me. But as soon as Archer came to a stop beside our row, Reynolds woke right up.

"Sorry, Doc." He yawned, stretching his arms above his head.

"Reynolds," I hissed under my breath when he moved to stand. I was not going to have another conversation like our first one with Luke on the team bus.

"You two have got some shit to clear up. I don't know what it's about or how you can fix it, but clear it up already." Reynolds slugged Archer's arm when he rose, then he lumbered down the aisle in search of a different seat.

Twisting around in my seat so I was angled toward the window, I tried to ignore the man standing in the aisle, watching me. I'd learned weeks ago that ignoring Luke Archer was impossible though.

"Are you going to sit?" I snapped under my breath when he continued to linger in the aisle. We were in the back of the bus and most of the team was more up front, but still. This wasn't exactly a private place.

"Are you going to talk?"

"I already said everything I need to talk about."

Luke slid into the seat beside me, his nearness taking me off guard. He shouldn't have still been able to make me feel this way. Not after everything.

"Will you listen then?"

"I'm stuck in the seat beside you," I answered, wondering what he thought he could say that would explain everything.

"What happened between us?" He twisted in his seat so he was almost facing me.

"I told you—we hit our expiration date. And there wasn't an 'us.' It was you and me coming together to have sex," I said quietly, glancing around to make sure no one was tuning into our conversation.

"I don't accept that. This wasn't *that* kind of a relationship."

"You don't have to accept it. It doesn't change the reality of it."

Luke's hand curled around his armrest, his knuckles fading to white from his grip. He might have been able to stay calm on the surface, but he wasn't inside. "I think you're mad at me about something. I think you heard something or read something or learned about something that made you feel like I'd betrayed you in some way. I'd like to know whatever it is so I can explain myself."

I shifted in my seat. "There's nothing to explain."

"Then there is something?"

My eyes closed. Why wouldn't he just let this go? Why was he acting like he really cared? I knew two months of the season were still left, but surely Luke Archer could get his physical needs attended to by no shortage of candidates. This unknowing, albeit welcoming, designated candidate was done.

"Let me give you my explanation since you've clearly arrived at your own." When Luke's arm bumped mine gently, warmth spread into my body. It should have been soothing, but my anger turned it into the opposite.

My eyes snapped open. "What is it you think you've done, Luke? What in the hell do you think you could have done to piss me off and push me away?" I paused just long enough for him to let that settle in. "If you won't accept that I'm through with us just because our fuck-buddy status ran its shelf life, then you must have something else in mind for why I called it off."

His brows came together as he inspected the area

around us like I had earlier. No one was twisting around in their seats.

"You keep asking me what's wrong and why I'm angry, so surely you must have come up with a list of reasons why. If you're asking me what it is you need to fix, then you must know there's something you broke in the first place." My whispered words were making me shake. "What do you have to explain to me, Luke?"

I saw something settle into his eyes, the creases of confusion ironing out. The longer he studied me silently fuming in the seat beside him, the more realization settled over him. He knew I knew.

I should have felt vindication in that. I should have felt victorious that I'd figured it out, unlike the ones before me. As I watched him fall back into his seat, his eyes closing and his mouth sealing, it felt like more of a defeat.

"See? You don't have anything to say either."

When I rose to find someplace else to sit, Luke's hand grabbed mine as I slid by him. As I felt my fingers start to curl around his, I swiped my hand away and bolted into the aisle.

"If you ever touch me again, I will tell everyone on this bus and everyone in the whole damn world about your little secret, Luke Archer." My voice shook as I glared at him. "Don't you ever lay your hands on me again."

Something dark flashed over his face, then he tipped his ball cap low on his face and closed his eyes. I guessed he was done fighting. I'd said what I needed to to make him give up. My threat hadn't made me proud—I knew the importance he placed on privacy—but it was all I had left to sever the connection he refused to let go of.

"How's that for pushing you away?"

chapter Twenty-Five

WE WERE BACK in San Diego for a home game. Home. I'd spent a lot of time thinking about what home was. Was it a city? A house? A person? A feeling? A combination of all of that?

Home. Most days it felt like a fantasy, something as lofty and far-fetched as a unicorn. Like you'd have to steal it if you really wanted it because it wasn't just going to fall into your lap. It wasn't a given; it was something you had to take.

As I sat at the small table in my apartment, I knew this wasn't home. It was so quiet, but not the kind that felt peaceful. The kind that felt lonely. The kind that made a person reflect on crazy things like the definition of home.

Just as I was straining my teabag, hoping chamomile might be up to the task of allowing me some sleep tonight, there was a knock on my front door. I wasn't expecting anyone and I hadn't had time to make any friends in San Diego who would feel comfortable enough to just swing by at nine o'clock at night.

When I glanced through the peephole to see who it was, I sucked in a breath. After the way things had gone down between Luke and me, I'd never expected to hear from any of his sisters again. Then again, I did remember the very one standing on the other side of my door warning me that if I hurt him, I'd have three sisters to answer to.

I guessed I didn't need to wonder why Alex was here.

Unlocking the door, I pulled it open. She returned my conventional smile, shifting like she was uncomfortable.

"Please don't tell me you drove all the way from Oceanside," I said softly.

She shook her head. "My sisters and I are staying with Luke this weekend."

I exhaled some relief before my next question popped to mind. "Does Luke know you're here?"

She shifted again. "Not *exactly*."

I exhaled. "Alex . . ."

"He wouldn't have let me come if I'd told him where I was going. I took a cab."

"You need to let him know. He will lose it if he finds out you're gone this late at night." Grabbing her arm, I pulled her into the apartment and closed the door. "You can use my phone."

"I've got a phone when I'm ready to call him, but first, I need to talk to you."

"Alex . . ."

"Luke has always taken care of me. Of all of us. I want to take care of him for once."

"And what does you being here with me have to do

with taking care of him?"

"Because he cares about you." She motioned at me. "I don't know what happened or why you guys aren't together anymore, but he's miserable and I need to know why. Since he won't say anything, I'm going to have to get it out of you."

I took a moment to consider my options. I could call Luke right now and drive her back to his place, or I could hear what she'd come here to say and then take her to his place. Judging by the look on her face, I'd probably have to throw her over my shoulder to get her into my car before she told me whatever she was here to say.

What was five minutes?

"This sounds like we're going to need chocolate." I sighed, wandering into the kitchen.

Alex followed. "Chocolate would probably be a good idea."

"Good thing I just stocked up," I said, pulling out the end time's stockpile of chocolate.

Alex's eyes went round. "The last time I saw this much chocolate was when my ex broke up with me." When she gave me a knowing look, I snagged a fun-size Twix from the stash. She took a seat on the barstool across from me, pulling a chocolate-and-caramel Kiss from the bag. "So why aren't you guys together anymore?"

I didn't answer until I'd finished my Twix. Just to see if the chocolate and sugar made it easier to talk about. "We weren't ever really together to begin with."

"Eh, yeah, you were," she replied, giving me a look.

"You saw us together once, Alex."

She popped the Kiss into her mouth and shrugged. "But I know Luke, and if you two weren't together, he wouldn't have let us see you together at all. He's never introduced us to anyone he's been with other than you." She was already fishing for her next piece when one side of her face pulled up. "Well, and . . ."

"Callie?" Okay, another piece of chocolate was in order after saying her name out loud.

"You know about her?"

"Yeah." I popped a few M&M's in my mouth, trying to cut the bitterness.

"Did he tell you?"

"No."

"Is that why you broke up with him?" She bit her lip, chewing something out on it. "Because if it was, I know why he didn't tell you."

I shook my head. "That wasn't the reason. At least not the main one."

Pulling her long braid around her shoulder, she studied me. Almost in the same way Luke had so many times. "What is the main one?"

"That's between Luke and me." A few more M&M's got dumped into my mouth. My plan of dulling the pain via chocolate was working. At least a little.

Alex was quiet after that. I wasn't sure if she was waiting for me to say something or trying to figure out what to say next. I felt bad that she'd come here and I couldn't be honest with her about the reason her brother and I hadn't worked out, but there was no way I could tell her the real reason. I didn't want to tarnish her view of her big brother.

After digging out a handful of Kisses, she started to make a little pyramid with them. She was on the second row when she glanced up. "Do you know about Owen too?"

I didn't know his name, but from the sound of her voice, I knew who she was referring to. "The little boy? Yeah, I found that out on my own too."

"That's why he didn't tell you about Callie—because of Owen. I know he would have eventually, but he doesn't tell just anybody about them."

At the same time I respected his decision to keep them private, given his world was what it was, I resented it. It was an immature reaction and I knew it, but it was the plight of the scorned lover.

"I can understand that," I said, trying to sound as convincing as I could. "It would be hard growing up being known as Luke Archer's son. All of the media. I get it."

Alex was just about to put the top Kiss on the pyramid when she flinched. The whole thing came crashing down. "Owen isn't Luke's son." She blinked at me. "Luke might have thought he was at first, but Luke isn't his father."

The package of M&M's dropped out of my hand. "What?"

Alex slumped in the seat as she unwrapped another Kiss. "I know. It's the worst. Callie got pregnant with Owen when Luke and her were together, so of course he assumed the baby was his." When Alex's eyes narrowed as she said Callie's name, I didn't miss it. "The whole time she was pregnant—even those first few weeks after Owen was born—Luke thought he was his. It's not like they were planning on getting pregnant, but he was going to do whatever it took to take care of them. You should have seen him, Allie." A sad smile touched her face. "God, he was such a great dad, you know? So proud—so in love with that little guy."

When her eyes got glassy, I knew mine would follow. I was a huge sympathy bawler.

"What happened?" I breathed.

Alex balled up her empty foil wrappers, her expression darkening. "Some asshole came into the picture before Owen turned one month old. Claimed he and Callie had been messing around for a while and demanded a paternity test." She snorted, shaking her head. "Turned out, the asshole was the father. Not Luke."

I had to lean into the counter for support. "Oh my god."

"It crushed him, Allie," she said. "Can you imagine thinking a child was yours, only to find out he wasn't and that the woman you loved had been going behind your back for months?"

"No, I can't imagine that." My mind was still reeling, trying to catch up, but then I realized Luke had been burned in the same way I had. Except Luke had it worse. "But I do know what it feels like to be cheated on."

Like she could feel my pain flooding my system, she dug out another Twix bar for me. "That little boy might be someone else's son, but Luke made sure he's taken care of. Owen has a nice college fund that'll pay for the best school in the country. And med school if he wants. And a starter home after."

My eyes were reaching max glassy levels before spillage ensued. If Alex shed a tear, I was a goner. "Does he get to see Owen very much anymore?"

She exhaled. "He hasn't gotten to see him in over two years. That woman and her asshole cut Luke out of the picture entirely. And since he had no legal rights to Owen, there was nothing Luke could do."

"Couldn't he have done something?"

"What? No judge is going to grant visitation rights to some guy who thought he was a kid's dad."

My shoulders slumped. "I guess not."

"Plus Luke came to realize that Owen's life would probably be more peaceful if he wasn't in it. It's not like the kid'll remember him, so it was really only for Luke's benefit that we wanted to keep seeing Owen. Not for Owen's."

I turned the Twix bar over in my hand, my appetite for chocolate gone. "He said that?"

"Of course he said that. It's Luke. He couldn't *not* do the right thing if someone threatened to end his baseball career."

I didn't know what to say. So much had just come at me that I couldn't remember why I had been so mad at him in the first place.

"I wish I would have known," I whispered. "What an awful thing to happen."

Alex's eyes met mine, the faintest glimmer of hope in hers. "Then you'll give him another chance?"

Another chance. If it had just been this coming between us, of course. If it had just been this, I probably wouldn't have called it quits. He couldn't control what others did to him any more than I could. We'd been burned, and we both had the scars to prove it.

Luke's and my issues ran deeper.

"This—Owen, Callie—they weren't the main reason we didn't work out."

She groaned. "Then what was?"

"It's complicated."

"Then let's uncomplicate it because I haven't seen Luke this happy in years. Not even with Callie before he figured out what a cheating whore she was."

"Wow. Fond memories?"

"Luke doesn't know I call her that. He wouldn't like it if he did." Her nose creased.

"Then we'll keep that our secret," I said, trying to figure out what was happening. Trying to figure out how it changed things, if it changed them at all.

"You've really never seen him so happy?"

Alex shook her head slowly. "Never."

"What about the other women after Callie?" I tried not to think about them—their pictures and their names—but I knew I'd never forget them.

Her forehead creased. "There haven't been any other women after Callie."

"That you know of."

She blinked at me. "That I know of *for sure*."

I glanced at her, trying to phrase this gently. "You just said Luke wouldn't introduce his sisters to someone unless they were serious. How do you know he hasn't had a mess of casual relationships?"

She made a face at me like she was questioning if I was serious. "Because Luke doesn't do casual relationships. And if he was, he would have told me. He wouldn't have introduced us, but he would have told me he was seeing someone."

My eyebrow peaked. "Because twenty-five-year-old brothers share all of their love life and interests with their little sisters?"

Rolling her eyes, she leaned up enough to pull her cell phone out of her back pocket. "This one does." Scrolling through her and Luke's texts, she stopped when she presumably found what she was looking for. "Read for yourself."

When I stalled before taking it, she set the phone in my hand and waved at it.

The date of the first one I saw was from a couple months ago.

Alex*: How's it going?*

Luke: *Great.*

Great? Alex sent first, followed by: *Who is she?*

Luke: *Am I that obvious?*

Alex: *Yes. Sooooo? Who is she?*

Luke: *Someone who doesn't know I exist.* I felt a ball form in my throat when I read his reply back to her. I knew he existed—I just hadn't known he'd acknowledged I did.

Alex: *You're Luke Archer. She knows you exist.*

Luke: *No, not this one.*
Alex: *Then let her know you exist.*
Luke: *How?*
Alex: *I don't know. What's she like?*
Luke: *Amazing.*

And now I was smiling. I kept scrolling through the conversation while Alex tore into a couple more chocolates.

Alex: *Amazing details?*
Luke: *She loves baseball.*
Alex: *Score.*
Luke: *She works harder than I do.*
Alex: *Impossible.*
Luke: *When she smiles, I can't breathe.*
Alex: *Better figure that out. Can't have you passing out from lack of oxygen. Won't impress her.*
Luke: *Good point.*
Alex: *Ok, so trouble breathing.*
Luke: *Check.*
Alex: *Heart palpitations?*
Luke: *Check.*
Alex: *Interruptions in sleep?*
Luke: *Check.*
Alex: *Smiling like an idiot?*
Luke: *Double check.*
Alex: *Yeah. You've got it bad.*
Luke: *I can't figure out a way to say hi to her without sounding like a moron.*

When I chuckled reading his text, Alex leaned over to see which one I was reading. She snorted. "It's a good thing he's so good at baseball, because that's the only game Luke's got."

Alex: *When you do say hi, make sure to invite me. I want to be there with popcorn.*

Luke: *She's an athletic trainer on the team.*

Alex: *Yikes.*

Luke: *I know.*

When I got to this last text, Alex scrolled through a bunch more, craning her neck until she found what she had in mind.

I think I blew it. was Luke's text to her.

Alex: *Impossible. But how?*

Luke: *My opening line. I bombed it.*

Alex: *Oh god. What did you say?*

Luke: *Whose ass do I need to kick, Doc.*

Alex: *This confirms it. You really are a moron.*

She shook her head with me as we shared another laugh. Then she scrolled down to almost the end of this seemingly endless stream of texts between Luke and her. Tapping the line she wanted me to start at, she leaned back into the stool again and waited.

Alex: *Thanks for the fun trip. We all approve of Allie.*

Luke: *Glad to hear it.*

Alex: *We like her.*
Luke*: Good. Because I love her.*

"And in case you think that's complicated, it isn't. It's pretty simple actually." Alex tapped the phone where his message was staring at me. "He loves you. If you feel the same way, whatever it is, you guys can figure it out."

I couldn't look away from the words on the screen. I couldn't stop thinking about what they meant. If that was true—if what Alex was saying was true—none of what Shepherd had said could be. Who did I trust? Luke and Alex? Or Shepherd? That was an answer that didn't require any contemplation.

What had I done? Why had I believed it so easily?

It didn't take long to realize why. Believing in the bad was so much easier than clinging to the good. My past had reared its ugly head and sabotaged a great relationship because of a failed one. I'd let my fear feed my insecurities until all it had taken was one drunken lie from one spineless man to ruin it all.

Up until this moment, I'd never realized how truly scared I was. Of not being taken seriously in my job. Of being cheated on again. Of being hurt and left again. Of being alone.

"Alex?" My voice was trembling from revelation overload.

"Yeah?"

"I made a mistake. A massive, colossal, unforgivable mistake."

She shoved over a few pieces of chocolate. "What do

you think I'm here for?"

"To make me answer for hurting your brother?"

She grabbed my hands and gave me a shake. "To help you fix it."

IF I SPENT all of my time worrying about finding the worst in a person, I'd never be able to see the best. That was one of the hundred things that had been floating through my mind after dropping Alex back off at Luke's apartment. He wasn't there, but Alex had told me where he would be. Where he liked to go when he had things to work out.

I'd been standing in the parking lot and watching him for a while. My sedan was parked next to his tank as I searched for the right thing to say to him. There were a million right things to say to him, a few things I should, and one thing I had to. I only hoped he'd be more receptive to having a conversation than I had been when he tried.

He was hovering at home plate of the field he'd played on in college. Luke had been one of the few players to earn a spot in the pros in the same city where he'd gone to college. I knew that had to do with him wanting to stay close to his family.

He's a good man. That phrase kept echoing through my head, a reminder of how many people had described Luke as such. Not just as a good baseball player or a decent guy, but as a good man. He'd lived up to that title again and again. From doing right by his sisters after their parents' death, to the whole ordeal with Owen, to the way he'd handled me even when I was being psycho.

The one in a million. He was standing right in front of me.

The bucket of balls he was hitting was getting low, and I couldn't miss my chance. I couldn't let fear mess things up one more time. I might have felt like I wasn't sure what to say or how to say it, but really, I knew. Alex had been right about life and love being simple. It was only when we tried to make things what they weren't, and morph them into something they couldn't be, that life got messy.

Shoving off from the front bumper of the same vehicle Luke had driven when he'd been a student here, I started for the field. The man made millions of dollars a year and he still drove that thing, not because it was what people expected of him but because it made him happy. I couldn't help comparing myself to that. Luke could have had his pick of millions of girls, but he'd chosen me. Not because of what the public would expect, but because it was what made him happy.

I was choosing what made me happy too. No more setting booby traps and guillotines to sabotage that.

The parking lot was a long way from the field, so he

couldn't have seen me pull up. From way back there, it would have been impossible to tell it was Luke Archer on that field, hitting ball after ball, the crack of his bat echoing into the night.

When the next ball sailed over the back fence, landing with a mess of others, I realized that maybe it wouldn't have been so hard to figure out it was Luke Archer after all.

For as hard of a time as he'd had connecting with the ball during the past two games, he was tearing it apart out here. Practically every ball he tossed into the air, his bat sent whizzing over the back fence.

Alex had said he'd spent a lot of time here after their parents died, that this was his way of working out problems and anger. I could see why. All of the lights stationed around the field were on, but no one was in the stands, no announcer was talking in the background, no ballpark smells filled the air. It was so quiet, just the crack of Luke's bat and his sharp grunt after each swing.

I'd never been on a baseball field like this, and somehow, it was even more magical than it was when it was brimming with players and fans, noises and smells.

Coming up to one of the entrance gates, I paused. It was locked. I wasn't sure how Luke had gotten in, but I wasn't going to let one locked gate stop me from doing what I had to. It had been a while since I'd climbed a cyclone fence, and it had been *never* since I'd climbed one this tall, but it only was ten feet of holey metal. If I couldn't tackle this, I had no right to assume I could tackle all of the other hurdles that would come in this kind of a relationship.

Slipping out of my shoes to make the journey easier, I tucked my shirt into my shorts and started climbing. The up was easy, the over scary, the down tricky, but I didn't try to make it something it wasn't. I was climbing a fence. That was all. I didn't need to think about the possibility of falling, of breaking my neck, of spending the rest of my life paralyzed, of any of the crap that would have kept me from doing it before.

Fear bled the love out of life. When there was an abundance of fear, there wasn't room for love to grow.

Fear had no place in my life anymore.

After hopping down on the other side of the fence, now barefoot, I jogged through the maze of concessions booths until I'd reached the stands. I walked up the third base line. His back was to me, his focus on nothing but the ball and his bat's connection with it. As another ball cleared the back fence by a large margin, it was impossible not to wonder if I was watching a legend in the making—one that would be remembered by generations.

Luke was in his standard jeans, sneakers, and T-shirt, his Shock ball cap settled into place. Watching him, feeling him close, made the ache start to spread inside me. It only grew the closer I moved.

I was passing third base when he froze just as he was about to toss another ball into the air. He didn't turn around; he didn't speak. He just stood there, rigid and with his back to me, waiting.

Say something, Allie. But don't just say something, say what you came here to say.

Before I could overthink it and second-guess what to say first, I shouted, "I'm sorry, Luke." When his stance seemed to go even more rigid, I kept going. If he planned on dealing with this the way I'd dealt with him when he'd tried talking to me, I didn't have much time to say what I needed to. "I messed up. So, so much, and I'm sorry."

I was halfway to home when Luke's bat lowered. "Sorry for what? That list could be pretty long from where I'm standing."

There was a sharpness in his words I wasn't used to, and he still refused to look back at me. That was fine, but I wasn't going to leave here before he knew. "For not communicating with you, for starters. I should have told you why I was so upset and given you the chance to explain."

Luke tapped the bat against home plate. "So you were upset about something? It wasn't just about our fuck-buddy shelf life expiring?"

My eyes closed. I'd made a mess by letting my fear drive me. "No, it wasn't about that. I had you paying for someone else's mistakes, just like you warned me not to do. I let my fears come between us."

Luke shook his head. "You let a lot of things come between us."

"I know." I stopped when I was still a ways back from where he was. To give him the space I could see he needed.

"You've been talking to Alex." He didn't voice it as a question.

"You knew?"

Alex had been so proud of herself, thinking she'd

given everyone the slip. The first time a seventeen-year-old had sneaked out of the house had been to go talk to her big brother's girlfriend to talk some sense into her. The "good" gene ran in the Archer family.

"I guessed where she'd run off to when I got the call from Cameron." For the first time, he glanced back to look at me. It was brief and there was no fondness in his expression, but it somehow managed to make me feel like nothing could really ever be wrong if I could just wake up to Luke's face every day. "I'm surprised you still have your hair. She wasn't very happy when she found out you broke up with me."

"I am too." I gave my ponytail a little pull. "But she gave me a second chance."

Throwing the ball still in his hand into the air, the empty ballpark echoed with the sound of his bat connecting with the ball. This one flew over the center field fence.

"She's always been the generous one in the family." He reached deep into the bucket for another ball.

"Will you do the same?" I asked, moving a step closer. "Give me a second chance?"

He was quiet for a minute, tossing the ball in the air and catching it. "Did she tell you about Owen?" He was trying to mask it, but the pain in his voice when he said his name was evident. "About what happened?"

I nodded, padding closer. The fine dirt of the diamond felt like cool silk beneath my bare feet. "Yes."

Luke stared at the center field fence, his eyes narrowing like he was somewhere else. Then his face cleared. "I was going to tell you," he said, turning so he was almost facing me. "I should have told you sooner, but it's a complicated story I don't share freely." As soon as his eyes lifted to mine, they flitted away. "I want you to know all of me, Allie, but I didn't want you to know all of me all at once. I wanted the good parts to shine first before the skeletons came falling out of the closet."

My chest ached, but it wasn't for me—it was for him. For everything he'd been through and everything he'd risen from. Losing both parents in one tragic night would have ended the careers of most players. Instead, he'd applied for guardianship of his three sisters and made his name a permanent fixture in professional baseball. And then that woman, the baby he'd thought was his—my heart didn't possess enough beats to throb for him. He could have smeared her name through the mud and cut the little boy off for good. Instead, he'd let the woman be and set up a college fund for the child.

"Luke," I said, my voice breaking. "You have nothing to explain. I understand all of it."

His head lowered. "I was just so desperate for comfort after my parents died, for some kind of companionship. I needed someone I could forget about the pain with for a while." The end of his bat tapped the sides of his sneakers. "My parents had the kind of relationship no one thinks is real, but they had it. Even as a kid, I knew my sisters and I had it good. I wanted what my parents had so badly that I was willing to overlook a lot to find it. I should have trusted my gut with Callie, but I let my desire to find true love justify fake love."

My hands wound around my stomach like I was trying to hold myself together. "I understand. You don't have to explain any of that to me. I get it."

"But I do have to. Don't you see?" His eyes lifted to mine and stayed there. "Because I want you to know all of me. Not just the good stuff, but the not-so-good too. I don't want you to know the pretend Luke Archer. I want you to know the real one. Because that's the Allie Eden I want to know too."

Flickers of hope were shooting through my veins. "Can you forgive me?"

"Allie." He exhaled, looking at me like he was surprised I even had to ask. "I forgave you before there was anything to forgive."

My body rocked from the sob I held back. "How can you say that?"

"Because forgiveness is part of a relationship." He took a breath and made his first step toward me. "Listen, I'm going to screw up. Everything from a simple mistake like forgetting to bring home milk to a serious fuck-up." His tongue worked into his cheek. "Like coming on way too strong from the start and making you think all I wanted was a fuck buddy."

"That's not why I thought that," I said. "I mean, yeah, you came on so strong you probably set a few records there too—"

"Can you forgive me for that?" The promise of a smile was in his eyes.

"Forgiven."

The smile started to spread, but then something seemed to hit him. "Wait. If it wasn't because of me coming on too strong, why did you think all I wanted was sex from you?"

"I didn't think that. Not really. Or not at first," I rambled.

"Not at first? So it was only after getting to know me that you started to think that?" Rightly so, Archer's face was creasing with confusion.

"No, sorry, this is harder to explain than I thought it would be."

His brow peaked. "Imagine trying to keep up with it."

"Someone said something to me," I tried again. "Something about you and why I was on the team."

He circled his bat at me. "Because you were the best person for the job?"

"You'd think, right? But no, that's not what I was told."

Luke's jaw stiffened. "What were you told?"

There was no easy way to put this. No gentle way to phrase it. "That I'd been hired to pretty much be your beck-and-booty-call girl. Oh, and after that main priority, to fill in as an athletic trainer."

Luke was quiet for a minute, his face a blank canvas. Then a few dark strokes of anger lashed across it. "And you believed it?"

I shifted. "This person made a convincing case. He brought up Callie, who'd been on board with the team your first season. The physical therapist the next season, and the dietitian last season."

His chest was moving fast, the grip on his bat turning his knuckles white. "Other than Callie, I barely knew those women. If they were some perk the Shock lined up for me, they failed to mention it in my contract because I sure as shit wouldn't have signed up for something like that."

"I know," I interrupted. "I know that now."

"But you didn't at first?"

My head bowed as I scuffed at the dirt with my toes. "No."

"Why?"

I made myself look at him. He didn't seem angry anymore, maybe just a little disappointed. "Because believing someone like you could only be interested in me for sex was so much easier than believing someone like you wanted the rest too."

His gaze roamed me before settling on my eyes. The look in them siphoned the air right from my lungs. "Someone would have to be the world's biggest fool to look at you and not want everything, Allie."

If it was capable of bursting from being overfull, my heart would have right then. "But everyone looks at you, Luke Archer, and wants everything. I'm just one of those millions."

Luke tossed the ball back into the bucket and started toward me, each step slow and purposeful. "No, everyone looks at me and sees a number, a team, stats. It takes a rare person to see the stubborn ass I can be at times and not walk away. A rare person to put up with this lifestyle, the schedule, my moodiness, and my seeming inability to hit the brakes once I get started. It takes a special person to see the real me and not be scared away."

"Rare? Another word for abnormal. Atypical. Unusual." I smiled as he approached me. "So are you saying I'm you're abnormal person?"

"Hell yeah, that's what I'm saying." When he was in front of me, he wound his bat around my back and pulled me to him with it. "And I'm your abnormal person too."

My hands lifted to his chest as he held me to him like he had the day of the photo shoot. The cool metal of his bat running across my back, the warm planes of his body spanning my front, the heat in his eyes made me weak at the same time it made me strong.

"Before I kiss you, before I do more"—his dimple pierced into his cheek—"I need to know who told you that."

"Why? Are you going to threaten to kick his ass too?"

He groaned, giving me a little shake. "Please don't bring up that first line fail ever again. It will haunt me to the grave as it is."

"I'll never bring it up again. Except for when I have to."

The lightness left his face as he held my stare. "Who was it?"

"Who do you think?"

"I know who I think, but I want to know if I'm right." He waited for my answer, not saying anything else.

One side of my face drew up. "Shepherd."

Luke's head fell back, a grumble vibrating in his chest. "That night at the charity event?" When I nodded, another sound erupted from his throat. "That son of a bitch. I saw you and him all up close to you, and I wanted to tear his throat out. If I'd known what he was saying to you, I actually would have."

My hand floated to the bend of his neck, trying to calm the anger I could see in his eyes. "Because nothing says charity auction like someone's throat getting ripped out, right?"

"He told you those other women were only on the team to warm my bed? That that was the reason you'd been brought on this season?"

My silence answered him.

"Anything else?" he asked.

I thought about everything Shepherd had said that night—everything I'd believed. Not anymore. "Not much. Just a few other stupid lies."

"God, Allie." Archer tucked me closer to him, tossing the bat away so his arms could hold me instead. "I wish you would have told me sooner. That night."

"I wish I would have too." My arms wound around his back, and I let him hold me so there was nothing between us.

"I wish you wouldn't have believed it."

My eyes closed as I turned my head into his chest. His heartbeat was thudding against my ear, so strong and sure. "Me believing that has very little to do with you, Luke, and more to do with me. I believed it because of my shortcomings, not because of yours."

Kissing the top of my head, his chin tucked over it afterward. "I'm sorry. So damn sorry. I'm going to make this right though. Shepherd's going to remember the day he went after the woman I love. He's going to be lucky if anyone lets him inside the gates of a baseball park as a spectator when I'm done with his lying ass."

Luke kept going, but I drowned out most of it after that first part. I'd read it on the screen of a phone, but it was entirely different hearing it from his mouth.

"I love you, Luke." My head lifted from his chest so I could look up at him. "You were right. You are more. *We* are more."

His hand left me just long enough to turn his ball cap around. "No," he said, then his hand molded onto my cheek as his face angled toward mine. "You're *everything*."

chapter Twenty-Seven

"SO HOW DID you get in here? Jump the fences with your bat and bucket of balls? Find the power switch to the stadium lights?" Looking up at Luke where we were still straddling the third base line, I waited.

His eyes roamed the empty stadium, looking sheepish. "I might have had someone let me in. The same someone who knows how to turn on the lights."

"Because this big, prestigious university is so generous to do that for any guy who shows up in the middle of the night wanting to hit a few balls on their pristine field?"

He sighed, knowing what I was hinting at. "The night guard might have season tickets to the Shock games." When my eyebrow stayed lifted, his shoulders slumped. "Box seat season tickets."

"Ah, so Luke Archer is not above bribery."

"Hey, for your information, he started letting me onto the field before the season tickets came into the equation. That was just my way of saying thanks."

"And no doubt that plays no factor in his willingness to continue breaking the rules for you." I blinked at him, my arms still tied around his back.

"Oh, please. The university doesn't mind."

"They said that?"

His arms tightened around me despite me giving him a hard time. "It's implied in the thank you note they send me every year for my considerable alumni donation."

"So you *are* above bribery?"

The corners of his mouth started to lift. "Bribery, yeah. But threats, not so much."

"For example?"

"For example, I'd threaten you."

My eyebrow lifted. "With what?"

"What do you think?"

"Then threaten me." Stepping out of his arms, my arms crossed in front of me and my fingers pulled at the hem of my shirt.

Luke wet his lips, glancing into the stands. After giving them a cursory check, his gaze moved back to me. "Take off your shirt or else . . ." His brows came together. "Or else . . ." He scrubbed his face, searching. "Or else *something*."

"Good enough for me," I laughed, pulling my shirt up and over my head. I tossed it at his face.

His hazel eyes went darker when they explored my body. "Take off your shorts."

When my fingers dropped to my button, I waited.

"Or else something."

Biting back a smile, I worked the button and zipper

free, then wiggled out of them until they were around my ankles.

"I like this game," Luke breathed, a grin stretching from one ear to the other. "I like this game a lot."

"Of course you do. We're playing it on a baseball field."

Like he was reminded of our environment, his eyes wandered back to the stands. They were empty. "Take off the rest," he ordered when his search was done.

My arms wound behind my back, waiting.

"*Or else* I'll tear them off myself."

"As tempting as that is, this is my favorite, and one of my only matching, bra and underwear, so I'll take care of the removal to keep things civilized."

"That's the only civilized thing you'll be having from here on," he growled, adjusting himself as I let my bra fall down my arms and onto the grass.

"Looking forward to it." I worked my underwear down as I kept moving toward him.

Now that I was all the way naked with one thing on both of our minds, he wasn't checking the stands anymore. They could have suddenly filled to capacity and he wouldn't have noticed, judging by the look on his face.

"You know we already made up, right?" He waved his finger between us.

"This isn't make-up sex." I shook my head, moving closer. "This is I'm-sorry-for-being-such-a-crazy-insane-nut sex."

Half of his face pinched together. "You were especially crazy."

"And I plan on especially saying I'm sorry for that."

Luke shifted. "*Saying?*"

My smile tipped up on one side. "Well, *expressing* just how very sorry I am."

"I am here for your expressing pleasure." He held his arms out and did a spin.

The moment he was facing me again, I leapt into his arms. He caught me like he was expecting it, his lips finding mine.

Luke kissed me softly for a minute, like he was trying to prove that even though I was naked in his arms and ready for the rest, he was content with and capable of just kissing. He spun me around slowly, the lights from the stadium seeming to wink down at us.

"I thought I'd lost you," he whispered as his forehead pressed into mine.

"No." I closed my eyes and breathed him in. "I just had to find myself again first."

Backing up until we were straddling home plate, his arms tightened around my back. "I need you, Allie." There was so much meaning behind those words, so much more than four words could ever hold.

"You have me," I promised.

"All of you this time?"

When my eyes opened, I found his waiting for mine. Trust was as much something you gave a person as they earned it. Luke had earned every bit of mine, and I was finally ready to give all I had. "All of me all of the time."

My answer was barely out before his mouth was on me again, but his restraint was gone. His hands lowered down my back to start working his pants loose, but the urgency of our mouths seemed to impair his coordination. He stumbled back a step but wasn't able to catch himself before we landed on the ground with a couple of surprised grunts.

"Shit, are you okay?" Luke dusted off my knees , which were still pinned around his lap, as he sat up.

My hands finished what his had started, lowering his zipper just enough to free him. I didn't slow down or take time to stretch out the moment. I needed him, all of him, but this part in particular right now.

When I slid down him, his head rolled back.

"I'm okay," I breathed, giving myself a second to enjoy the feeling of oneness. Sex with Luke had been many things, from filthy to redefining, but the one thing it had always been was transcendent.

Lifting, I slowly lowered my lap back over his. With a moan, he fell the rest of the way back. A small cloud of dust erupted behind him. His hands moved to my hips, gripping them as he moved below me. His hips thrust into me, making my body tremble with each thrust.

I was making love with Luke Archer in the middle of a baseball field. How did a person top this? But looking into his face as my body moved above his, I knew there'd be no end to these kinds of experiences. With someone like Luke, every day was an adventure. It was a journey I was looking forward to.

"This is the fucking best thing I've ever done in my life," Luke growled right before spinning me over so I was the one on my back. "But I want to be right here"—his face lowered to mine, his hips rocking into me from above, sending me closer—"looking into your eyes when I feel you come undone."

Curling his hand behind my side, he grabbed a chunk of my backside, riding me harder. "I want to be inside of you when I come." His other hand cradled my head to keep it from continuing to hit the ground. "Do you want the same?"

My head was dizzy from what he was doing to my body, but not lost enough to answer. "I don't want that, Luke." My words stilled his body, and I shook my head. "I *need* that. Always."

Something low echoed in his chest before he moved inside me again. Neither of us lasted long after that, his climax spurring mine. The entire time, his eyes stayed above mine, unwavering.

Only after our cries had receded and the silence had settled around us again did his eyes close. Leaning his forehead into mine again, I felt his sweat slide against my skin. He stayed deep inside me, like separating in that way would be the catalyst for waking up from the dream we'd found ourselves in.

"I have scored plenty of times on home plate, but this"—Luke's sweaty forehead left mine as he hovered above me—"*this* is a first."

My hands curled into his backside, holding him in place when he tried to shift his weight. "Is this a last?"

"Hell, no." Luke leaned up just enough to stare at me naked and spread out beneath him. "This is the start of a great tradition."

My hands formed around his face. “This is the start of a lot of great things.”

Chapter Twenty-Eight

THE SHOCK HAD made it to the big game. It had been one hell of a season, and this game had stayed with the same theme. It had come down to the last inning, the Shock and the Miners going back and forth leading the series. I'd never been so nervous watching a ball game, and I wondered if by the end of this, I'd have any functioning nerves left.

We were last at bat in the ninth, and we needed a run to tie. Two to win. Archer was next up with one on base.

After those two games where Archer had not been the number eleven fans had come to know, he'd come back with a vengeance. There wasn't a ball a pitcher could throw that he couldn't hit. He was back, but that wasn't all. He'd come back even better.

He'd already sent two balls over the fence this game—and we could really use a third.

"Why don't you run out there and give him one of those big kisses with that look in you women's eyes that says there'll be more of that to come if you hit a homer?" Reynolds sat down beside me in the dugout, taking a break from his pacing.

"I'm working, Reynolds."

"I know, I know. You're the team's athletic trainer first on game day, Archer's girlfriend second, but come on, Doc." Reynolds waved at the giant scoreboard that seemed to loom above the outfield. "This is the last inning of the last game of the biggest series in our lives. A little motivation couldn't hurt. Compliments of your lips and feminine guile."

"Feminine guile?" I blinked at him. "Who's spending their nights reading romance novels?"

Reynolds snorted. "The most action I see during the season is on those pages. I'll take what I can get."

I gave him a look that suggested conversation time was over, and I got back to focusing on number eleven's bat as he took a few practice swings before stepping into the box. After both of us had sat down with Coach to divulge our relationship—he'd basically responded that as long as it didn't affect our jobs, he could give a shit who we played footsie with—Luke and I went public. We knew it would get out sometime, and we both felt more comfortable having it come out the way we wanted instead of the way the press would spin it.

Luke had given a small press conference and started with mentioning that I was the best damn athletic trainer he'd had the privilege of working with. He followed that up with admitting I was the best damn woman he'd had the privilege of falling in love with. It was short and simple, and after the country had buzzed about Luke Archer's swoony confession, the story died down and life had gotten back to normal. Except now Luke and I shared a hotel room when we traveled, and we didn't have to worry about sitting next to each other at some team meal.

I loved not having to hide our relationship anymore. I loved how certain he'd been about wanting to announce it. I loved *him*.

I'd known this season would be life-changing. I just hadn't known it would be because I'd fall in love with a great man who would manage to help guide me through the minefield of my fears until we'd reached the other side.

Something else had changed after that night under the stadium lights—Shepherd had gotten his marching orders. Which was kind of ironic since he was the one who'd told me that's what I had to look forward to. Coach had been madder than a badger when he found out what had happened, and when Luke straight up told Coach he would not play on the same team as that kind of man, Shepherd was gone so fast most of the players didn't realize it for a few games.

The viper was gone, and even though I'd never let anything anyone said to me affect my trust in Luke again, it was a relief to not have to share space with Shepherd twelve hours a day.

"Hey, you wouldn't happen to have any cute, single, athletic training friends, would you?" Reynolds nudged me as he leaned forward. "I need an Allie Eden of my own."

My legs started bouncing. "None judgment-impaired enough to date you, Reynolds."

Reynolds's deep chuckle rocked his body. "If that was a qualifier, I'd never score another date again."

"Please, Reynolds, you know I love you"—I wiped my palms on my slacks—"but shut the hell up."

"I talk when I'm nervous."

My breath stopped when Archer crouched into position, the entire grandstands seeming to follow. "And I throw elbows when I am."

Reynolds shoved off the bench, getting back to pacing the dugout like he'd been the second half of the game.

The first pitch, Archer had to jump out of the box to keep from getting hit. Leaping from my seat, I had to bite back the string of curses the rest of the team were firing at the pitcher for taking a shot at one of their own.

The second pitch came in the same way. The sons of bitches were trying to walk him by beaning the hell out of him. They'd been trying to walk number eleven all night but hadn't sunk to this level yet.

When Luke stepped back into the box, he didn't throw a glare the pitcher's way like I was. He didn't give away that he was the slightest bit flustered. He just eased into the box, taking a different position than he normally did when he was at bat, and waited.

"That crazy bastard's actually going to try to hit one of those widowmakers."

My legs kept bouncing, silent prayers on my lips.

As the pitcher wound up, Archer made a last second adjustment, then the ball was whizzing toward him. It was high and inside again, but somehow Luke managed to connect with it. Everyone in the dugout rose to their feet, watching the ball sail into the outfield. It clinked off the wall of center field.

The dugout unleashed when Roberts made it to home, tying the game. Archer made it to second and nodded at us all while we continued to cheer like raving lunatics.

Mackey was up next and hit a line drive deep into right field, getting him safely to first and Archer to third. There were two on base as Hernandez moved up to the plate.

By now, I was standing with the rest of the team, leaning out over the dugout, ready to split open from the tension. From third base, Archer glanced into the dugout, his gaze stopping on mine. From the slant in his smile alone, I knew what he had in mind.

I thought back to that conversation we'd had months ago, when I'd told him not to do it, that it was too risky. This time, I gave him my nod of approval. His smile widened as he leaned over to whisper something to the third base coach. After a little back and forth, I could see that Archer had gotten his way. He usually did in my experience. A team didn't typically advise a runner to steal home with runners on base, but with their two strikes on the board and being tied at the bottom of the ninth, it became more appealing. Hernandez was one hell of a shortstop, but not the hitter you wanted up in this kind of a situation.

The moment the pitcher wound up, I held my breath and didn't let go. Archer started pulling away from third, every muscle in his body primed for a burst of adrenaline. When the pitcher noticed Archer creeping off third, Archer feinted back to third, just enough to entice the pitcher into trying for the out. As soon as the pitcher threw the ball to the third baseman, Archer hauled ass to home.

The entire stadium lunged onto their feet, their shouts pumping onto the field. Hernandez backed away from the plate as the third baseman fired the ball at the catcher. Luke lunged back for third, the catcher whipping the ball back to his teammate. On it went for what felt like an eternity, Luke getting closer to home, while the Miners' catcher and third baseman got closer to him.

There was a reason players didn't steal home anymore. It was next to impossible to do. That was the reason Luke wanted to do it so badly. He didn't believe in impossible. He didn't let the odds scare him. He didn't let the fear of failing keep him from trying.

He lived life the same way he played baseball.

When the ball smacked into the third baseman's mitt again, Archer went for it. His legs a blur of movement, he powered for home plate, his elbows stabbing into the air behind him. No one was bouncing and shouting in the dugout anymore —everyone was silent.

Archer flew into the air as the ball careened back to the catcher looming over the plate. It was going to be close. The ump was in position, not daring to blink as both the ball and Archer's body sped to home plate.

He exploded down on home, dust erupting all around him as his momentum sent him barreling into the catcher, who'd just caught the ball and was swinging his glove onto Archer's back.

I was still holding that same breath while everyone waited for the call that seemed to take forever to be shouted.

The moment the ump waved his arms out at his sides, I started screaming. So loudly I didn't even hear him yell safe.

He'd done it—he'd stolen home.

Luke Archer had done more than that though. He'd stolen my heart too.

As the fans went wild, the Shock charged the field. Typically the support staff didn't rush a field with the team, but there was nothing typical about what had just happened. Weaving into the mix, Reynolds cleared a path for me up the stairs so I didn't get trampled. Once we hit the field, Reynolds grabbed me. I somehow ended up on his shoulders as he charged toward the swarm of bodies at home plate.

Luke had just been tossed up onto a couple of his teammates' shoulders and was throwing his hands toward the stadium, only fueling the fans' excitement. Somewhere in the midst of it all, he'd lost his batting helmet, so his damp hair was bouncing as the guys holding him leapt beneath him.

Reynolds and I were charging down the third base line when Luke's head turned. A dozen emotions played on his face, a dozen more lighting up his eyes, but there was only one I felt when he looked at me like he was now—like I was the only person in this sold-out stadium. Like I was the only person in the whole world.

The stadium was roaring with noise, a flurry of scenes vying for attention, but I didn't miss what he shouted as he lifted his arm and pointed in my direction. *For you.*

Reynolds's impressive size made cutting through the crowd a reality I never could have managed on my own. He somehow managed to barrel right through the mess of players until Luke and I were within arm's reach.

Luke was grinning at me like he'd just challenged the world to a duel and come out the victor. Holding out his hand for mine, when I placed it in his, he stabbed our combined hands into the air. The noise shaking the stadium grew louder as what felt like millions of lights blinking at us from the stands flashed all around us. It was a beautiful sight—the reaction of thousands of fans to Luke Archer stealing home plate to win the biggest game of any player's life.

I'd never forget it.

But as I glanced back over at Luke, who was still staring at me, I knew the sight in front of me now was the most beautiful one I'd ever seen. The one I'd always remember. The way the man I loved was looking at me when everyone else was looking at him.

I didn't just see a future when I looked at Luke—I saw the explanations of my past. The answers to the hurt. It had brought me to this very moment, molding me into the person I was today—the person Luke Archer loved.

His love was worth the price I'd paid in my past. His love was worth any price.

It was priceless.

epilogue

"YOU KNOW WHAT seeing you in my jersey does to me," Luke greeted as he kicked the front door closed, his arms loaded with grocery bags.

"I'm also in cut-offs and sneakers." I fought a smile as I washed tomatoes for the burgers we were grilling tonight.

"So? All I see is my name on your back and it does things to me . . ." Dropping the bags on the counter, he swung around the island until he was behind me. His arms wound around my waist, his body pressing into mine—a certain part of it pressing into my backside. "And depending on your mood, it does very good or very bad things to me."

The tomato dropped into the sink, my hand melting beneath his touch. I tried to fight it—the feeling of being utterly and totally under his spell—but I failed every time. Luke and I had been together for a while now, and after all of this time, he still touched me like it was our first and kissed me good night like it was our very last.

"This jersey that's got you so worked up also has spit-up on it from earlier." I tipped my head back to look up at him, tying my fingers through his hands. "Still all hot and bothered?"

His head nuzzled mine, his hips pinning me to the counter. "You have no idea how much of a turn on spit-up can be on the woman who gave me the most beautiful baby in the whole damn world."

As I laughed, I checked the clock on the wall. The same wall Luke had hung the framed cover of the two of us on *Sports Anonymous*—thankfully, I'd talked him out of hanging it on every wall in the house. We had ten minutes until people were supposed to start arriving. I might have preferred a bigger window to enjoy my husband's body, but I knew from experience we could make ten minutes work.

"If you can make it quick, you're on."

I hadn't finished my sentence before he had me spun around, his fingers already working on my cutoffs. "You don't steal home without being quick, Mrs. Archer. I think I can manage."

My hand had his shirt just about over his head when we heard it. Luke and I shared a groan.

"Built-in radar, that one," I said, pulling his shirt back over his head before heading toward the nursery.

"I've got her." Luke grabbed my hand before I could get far. He dropped a kiss on my forehead before jogging down the hall.

"If you think she's got you in the palm of that tiny

hand of hers now, just you wait, Luke Archer," I hollered down the hall after him.

He chuckled as he disappeared in the room across from ours. "In her palm, in your heart, I'm a happy man."

The baby monitor was propped on the counter in front of me, but I didn't turn it off. I kept it on because I loved witnessing these private moments between Luke and our daughter.

"Afternoon, sunshine. Did you have a nice nap?" Luke came into view as he leaned over the crib, which made Lily's little legs start kicking like crazy, her face lighting up from seeing her daddy. "Let's get you up and ready for the party. And holy . . ." Luke said as he picked up Lily. "For something so sweet, you stink something fierce."

They went out of view, but I could still hear them moving around the room.

"Wait. Maybe I'm not supposed to say that you stink. You know, in case you remember it in some strange memory one day, and it gives you a complex that your dad said you stunk." The sound of diaper tape being ripped open was followed by a grunt from Luke. "Holy . . ." His voice was muffled from probably plugging his nose. "You are one sweet, *sweet* baby, Miss Lily Archer." The muffled voice thing was gone, probably because he was worried the image of him pinching his nose while he changed his six-month-old baby's diaper would give her some kind of a permanent mental scar.

After that, a couple of made-up songs about baseball, sung to the tune of "Twinkle, Twinkle Little Star," were accompanied by Lily's coo-giggle while they finished up. I got back to cleaning the last couple of tomatoes, not able to help the happiness that flooded my system.

I thought my dreams had come true the day I'd been hired on by the Shock—I never hoped to imagine there could be anything better than landing my dream job. But there had been. There'd been lots of so much better things. Like meeting Luke. Falling in love with him. Slaying a legion of demons on my journey toward doing so. Getting engaged. Being married. Having a baby.

Just when I was sure it couldn't get any better, life did. It still came with its challenges—as was life's nature—but navigating them with the person I loved made them feel smaller somehow, not so impossible to conquer. Our schedules were still exhausting, and having a baby going into spring training would make them that much more. But it was worth it. Anything would have been worth being with them.

Luke and Lily were dancing down the hall while Luke hummed a classic waltz melody—"Take Me Out to the Ball Game"—when the doorbell rang.

"Party face time." Luke gave Lily a serious face as they detoured toward the door.

Lily gave him a serious face back. That lasted for all of half a second before she was grinning and flapping her chubby little arms.

"Nice party face, kiddo. That's my girl."

Grabbing a towel to dry my hands, I moved toward the front door with them. I knew who it was before I'd made it around the corner to see who had shown up first—

from the sound of Lily's shrieks alone.

"Sisters! Aunties! Welcome, welcome." Luke swung the door open to let his three sisters in, trying to pull the first into a hug.

Alex swept around him with Gaby and Cameron, already pulling Lily out of his arms.

"Hey. Great to see you too." Luke's face flattened as he flashed a wave at the girls' backs. "Do I have to hang Coach bags and chocolate truffles off of me to get some love again?"

If they heard him, they didn't respond, already fawning all over Lily.

"Hey, girls," I said as they moved into the living room.

"Hi, Allie."

Cameron smiled and Alex gave me a quick side hug as they passed.

From the door, Luke's mouth was hanging open, making him look all dejected. "I give them a niece and they don't need me anymore."

Holding out my hand for him, I tipped my head toward the kitchen. "Well, I need you. Manning the grill."

"At least someone still needs me," he said loudly enough to echo through the house. Still nothing.

"Oh my gosh, Luke!" Cameron's head whipped toward her brother.

He started to smile, mollified someone had acknowledged him.

"Really? A Shock onesie? That's cruel."

I hadn't noticed what Luke had changed her into after

her nap, but now that I did, I smiled.

"What? I put her in one of those frilly tu-tu things and a matching bow headbandy thing too. She looks adorable." Padding up to where the girls were falling onto the couch, Luke motioned at Lily like she was perfect in every way. Which she was. Her present outfit included.

"She's a girl. Wearing a baseball onesie."

Luke crossed his arms. "She's a girl whose dad plays for the team her onesie's pimpin'. It's perfect."

When he glanced at me for support, I pinched the Shock apparel of my own I was "pimpin'."

Like she had to get her own say, Lily glanced at what her three aunts were scoffing over. Her face did that serious thing where you could tell she was thinking, staring at the Shock's emblem stitched across it. Then she patted her stomach, grinning and pushing off against Alex's legs like she approved.

"That's my girl." Luke thumped his chest a few times at Lily before heading out to the deck. "Gotta get my grill on before the rest of the guests arrive."

"How many more people are coming?" Alex asked, not minding when Lily started yanking at the long necklace she had on.

I rushed back to the kitchen from just thinking about it. "Oh, just the entire team and their families."

The girls followed me.

"Why everyone all at once? Wouldn't it have been easier to do a few smaller get-togethers?" Alex handed Lily off to Cameron to help me pull food out of the fridge.

"Probably, but Luke wanted a house warming party,

not a get-together."

"Does Luke always get what he wants?" Alex started peeling Saran Wrap off of the salads I'd made to go with the burgers tonight.

I smiled at her as I set out the condiments. "Only if I can help it."

"I hope he knows how lucky he is to have you."

That was when he glanced inside the slider doors from where he was scrubbing the grill. That look hadn't changed. The one that made me feel like there was only him and me and endless possibilities.

"He does," I replied, letting my eyes linger on his for another moment. "And I know how lucky I am to have him."

SIX HOURS LATER, we'd finally kicked out the last of the guests. A mess of empty beer bottles and soda cans were strewn around the house, dirty dishes stacked in the sink, the leftovers of a good time piled all around.

After checking on Lily, I wandered into the living room, expecting to find Luke passed out, probably still with his shoes on. Instead I found him at the kitchen sink, washing dishes.

I should have known.

"Did you enjoy the party?" I asked as I came up behind him, yawning.

"I did enjoy it." He tipped his head back at me and gave me a kiss as he continued to scrub the plate he was working on.

"I have a feeling you're going to enjoy even more what I have planned to end the party." My hands come around his waist, one lowering just enough to discover he was already on the same wavelength.

The faucet turned off. "Yeah?" he said from deep in his chest, slowly turning around.

Looking up, I spun his ball cap around and stared at my husband. He was the best thing to ever happen to me. He'd shown me love and given me Lily. He was a professional baseball player, and I was an athletic trainer on the same team. We'd both been burned to the marrow in our own ways, yet risen above the ashes to find each other.

Luke Archer might have been the one who'd stolen home plate, but I'd stolen my own kind of home. Because sometimes you had to fight for the things you wanted. Sometimes you had to steal the life you wanted before fate realized you were coming. I'd stolen home too, and it was one for the record books.

"We had a one-in-a-million chance of making it, you know that, Luke Archer?" My hands curled around his neck as he pulled me tighter to him.

His dimple curved into his cheek before he threw me over his back and carried me down the hall toward our bedroom. "Never tell me the odds."

The End

Thank you for reading STEALING HOME
by NEW YORK TIMES and USATODAY
bestselling author, Nicole Williams.

Nicole loves to hear from her readers.
You can connect with her on:

Facebook: Nicole Williams (Official Author Page)
Twitter: nwilliamsbooks
Blog: nicoleawilliams.blogspot.com

Other Works by Nicole:

CRASH, CLASH, and CRUSH (HarperCollins)

UP IN FLAMES (Simon & Schuster UK)

LOST & FOUND, NEAR & FAR, HEART & SOUL

FINDERS KEEPERS, LOSERS WEEPERS

COLLARED

THE FABLE OF US

THREE BROTHERS

HARD KNOX, DAMAGED GOODS

CROSSING STARS

GREAT EXPLOITATIONS

THE EDEN TRILOGY

THE PATRICK CHRONICLES

CPSIA information can be obtained
at www.ICGtesting.com
Printed in the USA
BVOW03s1844240717
490140BV00001B/91/P